Praise for

D.J. Manly

Schism is a very good story about discovery, acceptance, tenacity and love…D.J. Manly gives us many great characters in this story…a great read. ~ *Blackraven Reviews*

I0616943

Total-E-Bound Publishing books by D.J. Manly:

Gladiators
House of Simeon

Anthologies:
Stealing My Heart: Stealing Rain

SCHISM

D.J. MANLY

Schism
ISBN # 978-0-85715-084-4
©Copyright D.J. Manly 2010
Cover Art by Lyn Taylor ©Copyright 2010
Interior text design by Claire Siemaszkiewicz
Total-E-Bound Publishing

Published in 2010 by Total-E-Bound Publishing, Think Tank, Ruston Way,
Lincoln, LN6 7FL, United Kingdom.

SCHISM

Dedication

This book is dedicated to one of my fans...Sabrina Beach, who inspired this story.

Chapter One

His father hadn't said much during supper, but then, that was his style. He was a man of few words, but the faint smile on his face at supper had spoken volumes.

"He's very happy, very proud of you. We both are." His mother reached up and placed a hand on his shoulder.

"I know," Sundar muttered. *But damn it all, would it kill him to say it once?*

"You're staying for dessert, right?"

"No," he said, "I can't. I've got to get back. I've got a pile of paperwork that needs doing." He reached down and pecked her on the cheek. "Meal was great, as usual." His gaze strayed to the window for a moment where he could see his father walking a grey mare around the corral outback. "How's Wildfire doing?" He shrugged into his waist-length leather coat and zipped it. It was getting nippy out there. He could smell winter in the air.

"Better. She's always going to be lame. Your father doesn't want to accept that. She's his favourite."

"I know." She was his favourite too. He'd been only nine years old when his father had bought her. He'd fallen in love with her. Wildfire was now approaching her eighteenth year. But that wasn't so old when he thought about his grandfather's horse. Misty had lived to be twenty-six.

"You look far away," his mother said suddenly, caressing his thick black hair between her fingers. "You don't need to cut your hair now, do you?"

"Naw," he grinned, "one of the perks of making detective."

"Good, it suits you long. Your father wore his long when we met, down to his waist almost. I used to love to brush it. You know, I was just thinking, we never get to see that girl you're dating. What's her name again, Maria?"

"Huh?" He gave her a dazed smile, watching his father gently stroking Wildfire's mane.

"That young woman you brought to your cousin's wedding last summer. She really liked you." She was waiting for an answer.

He headed for the door. "We aren't seeing each other anymore. She, ah...moved away, got a better job and—"

"Sundar?"

His hand was on the door handle. *Don't mention fucking grandchildren again.* He turned and glanced at her over his shoulder. "Yeah?"

"You're twenty-five years old. All your cousins are married or settled down now. You work too much. You got your promotion, try and make some time for..."

He pushed the door open. "Say goodbye to Dad."

"You're too much of a playboy," she called after him, laughing as she stood huddled in the door. "Living up to your name? I regret calling you Sundar now."

Sundar opened the car door and slid into the driver's seat. He waved at his mother, fired up the engine of his vintage 1969 Camaro, and careened out of the gravel driveway.

If he had a dollar for every time his mother said she regretted naming him Sundar, he'd have already paid off this baby he was driving. Sundar was his Tsalagi name, Cherokee to white folk. It meant lover, but God forbid some of his colleagues find that one out. He'd never live it down. Anyway, everyone called him Sunny. It was kind of a joke because he'd never had what you'd call a sunny disposition.

His mother, Sophia Macgregor, was of Italian-Irish descent. She was full of life and energy, and she'd given him some wonderful memories growing up. His father, Clinton Kingfisher, whose native name he'd never told anyone, was a full blooded Tsalagi who'd left the reservation young, worked in a garage and studied to become a mechanic. At the age of twenty-five, he opened his own garage and had three others working for him. He'd made a good living for himself and his mother, but he refused to embrace his own heritage, telling Sundar that being an Indian would get him nowhere in life. "You can't beat 'em," he said, "so join 'em. They call you Sunny, let 'em. Makes them feel better about who you are, lets them treat you like an equal."

His parents were polar opposites. His father was quiet, brooding, a man of little words, whereas Sophia was a social butterfly, volunteering with all kinds of organisations and feeding the penniless strangers who sometimes drifted through town. Sofia and Clinton could have been on a poster for 'opposites attract,' but yet they were hopelessly devoted to one another.

His mother had tried in vain to get his father to have some pride in who he was, and insisted on giving their only son a truly Tsalagi name. She wanted her only son to know about his native background, and when Clinton refused to take him to visit his grandfather, Sophia took him herself.

His grandfather seemed to live hundreds of miles away and yet, his mother had told him, it was only fifty miles. The old man spoke only Iroquoian and frowned at him when he spoke English. As a result, Sundar had learned the language and some of the native ways, including how to hunt and fish. His father never asked about those visits and Sundar never offered to tell him. It's just the way it was.

As he drove slowly along the downtown streets of Raleigh, the sun was dipping lower in the sky. It was getting darker earlier now and the leaves had all left the trees. He found this part of the year very depressing.

He pulled into the parking lot of the downtown precinct and regretted not staying later last night to finish up his paperwork. He could be home now watching sports on TSN. As he walked into the semi-lit squad room, a cheer went up, and he stepped back in surprise. "Hello, Detective!" someone shouted out, and then he heard the top popping off a bottle of champagne. "Hey, Sunny," the captain walked out of his office to greet him with a big grin, "we've been waiting for you."

Sundar narrowed his eyes, becoming aware way too late that he was about to get doused with a bottle of champagne. There was laughter as Norman Jacobs, one of the other detectives, jumped up like a basketball star and tipped a full bottle of the liquor over his head. It plastered his hair against his head and dripped off his leather jacket.

Sundar tightened his mouth into what might have been a smile and extended his tongue over his lips to lick the champagne. Then he started to laugh.

* * * *

Xander tried not to sound impatient. Mrs. Clifton was always like this, but damn it, it was almost closing and he had plans. "I'm not sure," she said, glancing at him. "Did you like me as a blonde, Xander?"

"Yes," he said, trying to sound super enthusiastic. "You looked ten years younger. This is a nice shade," he picked a box of ash blonde off the shelf.

"But it won't be that colour on me, will it? I shouldn't have gone golden brown last month. Why didn't you stop me?"

"I, ah…well," he muttered, "I didn't even know you went golden brown. Did you do it yourself?"

"No, Kathy did it over at the hairdresser's. She should have known better."

"Do you want me to slap her?" It was a joke, but one that didn't come off well. And suddenly he noticed that the pharmacist was standing there.

"Hello, Mrs. Clifton," Barbara Donaldson said. "Is everything okay?"

"Oh yes, Xander was helping me choose another colour. I get so bored."

"You could always go red," Xander said.

Barbara gave him a look.

Damn it, it's nine o'clock. "Well, maybe not red, auburn?"

"Auburn," she mused. "You know what?"

"What?" He was waiting with baited breath.

"Maybe."

He swore inwardly.

"I'll come back. I'm feeling pressured." She put down the box she was holding and left the drug store.

Barbara was looking at him.

"What?"

"Xander. Red? The woman would look like a vampire with red hair."

"Vampires are in." He grinned then winced when she scowled at him.

"Lock up the back. You want a ride?"

"I got a ride," he smiled, in more ways than one.

Barbara peered out the front window and made a face. "Not with that guy again. Your brother says he's a degenerate."

Xander shrugged. "He thinks all my boyfriends are degenerates."

"Where are you going tonight?"

"Barb," he said as he locked up the cash, "I'm going to be twenty-one tonight at twelve midnight. You guys should try to stop acting like overprotective mother hens."

"We stopped doing that when you were eighteen."

"Yeah, right!"

"Oh, and does that mean you'll be getting your own place?" She raised an eyebrow. There was a slight grin.

"When I graduate."

She placed a hand on his back. "I don't know why you don't go in to be a pharmacist."

"I'd have to live with you guys a lot longer," he threatened. "The certificate takes six months, a pharmacist, forever. You choose."

"Never mind, be a…what is it again you're taking?"

"Hotel management." He'd told her a hundred times.

"Right. In my day you didn't have to go to trade school to wait on tables."

"You're a snob, Barbara. I wouldn't be waiting on tables."

She nodded. "Are you still babysitting for us tomorrow night?"

"I said I would, even if it is my birthday."

"Every day is your birthday, kid," Barb shut off the light and they walked out the front door. "Alarm on?"

"Yep. Bye." He raised a hand and hurried over to the car where David was waiting.

"That your sister-in-law?" David asked as Xander jumped in beside him.

"Yeah, that's her."

"She looks like a bitch."

Xander glanced at him. David had a stud coming out of his lip, and one in his eyebrow, that one was new. His hair was multicoloured, a little passé, but David was good at giving him what he craved, for now. "Only I can call her a bitch. Let's go. I want to get to Raleigh before the club gets too packed."

"It's only a half hour away, Xan. And don't you want to fuck first?"

"No, I want to be in a crowd of beautiful, naked, sweaty men. The fucking can come later."

He shrugged. "Whatever," he muttered and turned up the volume of some heavy metal group screaming out lyrics.

Xander watched the streets of Cary float by, realising that when he came back through this town later, he'd be twenty-one years old. Although, he'd really always felt old, even as a kid. He'd been in the custody of his older half brother, Nathan, since their parents had been killed in a car accident six years before. Nathan was fifteen years older, and worked as a road work supervisor for Wake County. His wife, Barbara Donaldson, was the local pharmacist. They had a year old baby named Sarah. Barbara had given him a job in the pharmacy as soon as he'd graduated high school. She wasn't a bad person. She was just uptight, coming from a rich, conservative family who had no use for people unless they were exactly like them. She put up with him because of Nathan and, most of the time, treated him with civility. Deep down, she probably even cared for him.

When the city districts of Raleigh came into sight, Xander breathed easier. He always felt better in the bigger city, surrounded by people who didn't give a damn who or what you were. As soon as he finished his certificate in hotel management, he was moving to Raleigh, and planned to get a job in one of the classier hotels. Maybe one day he'd even have his own restaurant.

The Cave was a clandestine club not far from the downtown core. The gay club catered to a variety of tastes, and contained a number of different rooms where one could go to enjoy such things as BSDM, both heavy and light. Xander was out of David's car as soon as he'd parked it. He allowed David to throw an arm around him and they walked steadily towards the unmarked entrance. This was his night, and he had no intention of letting anyone or anything get in the way.

Someone was stroking his hair. He heard his name being spoken softly then a little louder. "Sunny?"

His eyes snapped open and he picked up his head. Damn it. He'd fallen asleep filling out these stupid forms. "Joyce?" he blinked, looking up at her. She'd made detective three years ago. She was a damn good cop, recently divorced, and completely devoted to the job.

She laughed. "You look like a small boy. And you smell like champagne."

"Still?" he grumbled. "I thought the shower would take care of it."

She shook her head. "I take it the reports weren't too stimulating?"

He stretched his hands over his head and yawned. "Not really."

"You're going to hate me."

"What?"

"We got a call about an underground club called Cave. Ever heard of it?"

Sure, he'd heard of it. "No. What about it?"

"We got a call from a man, said that they got his underage son in that hole. Imagine," she scoffed, pouring a cup of coffee, "it's not enough with what those freaks are into in that place, they got to be doing it with kids too."

"Want me to stop by on my way home?"

"Would you?" She handed him a slip of paper. "You'd be doing me a big favour. I'm beat. Anyway, the minor's name is Phillip Reynard. He's sixteen. Probably not even there anymore."

"Got a description?" he stood, his six foot six frame dwarfing hers.

"Not a very good one. I wrote down on that paper what the father told me. He didn't want to come down with a photo. Kid is mature looking for his age, about five ten, one sixty pounds, blond hair, and blue eyes. You could stop by the house and ask for a photograph before you…"

"No, I'll find the kid."

"We should call a raid on that joint."

"Why?"

She stared at him. "Because it's illegal for one thing and now with the minor incident, it's…"

"What's the owner's name?"

"Robert Houser."

He nodded. "I'll handle it, but you're doing the paperwork." He picked up his jacket, checked his watch. It was a little after ten.

The lights were dim in the office, only a handful of police working quietly at their desks. Joyce came closer. "My invitation for dinner is still on, by the way."

He nodded.

She put a hand on his forearm, met his gaze. "Why don't you drop by after you get done with the minor, and have a coffee at my place? I'll make you breakfast?" She tilted her head and licked her shiny glossed lips. One of her hands flattened against his chest.

"I, ah…I'm a little tired but I'll try."

She nodded and took a step around. "That last time was fantastic."

Sundar didn't comment. He just headed out the door, feeling the pockets of his jeans for his car keys as he did.

He got into behind the wheel of his car and slowly rolled out of the parking lot. Sex had been okay with Joyce, but not great. It wasn't her fault. He'd yet to have what he could remember as being great sex. It was odd how his partners always raved about it afterwards but yet it never left much of an impression on him. He hadn't found the secret ingredient yet.

As The Cave came into view, he pulled over to the side of the road and sat there staring at the unmarked door. He'd heard people talking about this place, and it had piqued his interest; gay men of every shade, finding exactly what they needed in this place. There was nothing wrong with that, he guessed.

He got out of his car and slammed the door. This shouldn't take too long. Joyce was going to owe him one. He walked across the street, his tall, broad shouldered profile casting a long shadow across the pavement. He'd played ball in high school, been scouted too by the major league. He could have gone all pro if a rival player hadn't slammed into him so hard that it had shattered his kneecap. Oh well, he didn't think that anymore. Those days are over. And he liked his job, and even more so now that he didn't have to wear the uniform and his pay packet had increased. No more traffic detail, he thought to himself ironically, just pulling minors out of underground homosexual clubs at the end of his shift.

He pulled open the door and was bombarded with a blast of music from the eighties. He made his way down a pair of rather steep steps and found himself looking into the eyes of a beefy, half-naked door man who stood almost as tall as he did.

Sundar flashed his badge.

"Oh no, the heat," he groaned. "And so hunky too."

"I'd like to speak to the manager," he said.

"He's inside. And we are completely above board."

"You have a minor in here, maybe more than one. Do you check ID?"

"Of course," he muttered.

He was lying. "Yeah, right," Sundar laughed.

"It's ten dollars — entrance fee." He raised his chin.

Sundar laughed at him and walked past. He stood just inside the entrance and looked around. There was a huge bar surrounded by men drinking, a multitude of tables spread around, and a dance floor packed with shirtless men strutting their stuff. Off from the bar was a corridor. That was most likely where the rooms were, rooms where a smorgasbord of sexual activities went on.

Several men walked by him, giving him the once over. "Come on in, honey, just don't stand there," a voice said suddenly.

Sundar glanced at the man at his side. "Ah, the manager, do you know where he is?"

"There, at the bar—he's playing bartender. He's a lucky guy if you're looking for him."

Sundar ignored that and walked over to the bar. He motioned to the man serving drinks.

He walked over, a middle-aged man with a bald head. "Well hello there, baby. Haven't seen you before. What can I get you?"

"You Houser?"

"Yes." He narrowed his eyes.

"Detective Kingfisher." He flashed his badge. "Is there someplace we can talk?"

He threw down the dishtowel he had in his hand. "Sure," he said.

He came out from behind the bar, and Sundar followed him down the hallway and into a small office. Sundar closed the door.

"If you're coming to harass me, think better of it," he pointed. "We're doing nothing illegal here. What's illegal is this fucking harassment by you self-righteous…"

"Whoa, whoa," Sundar held up a hand, "calm yourself, Mr. Houser. I'm not here to shut you down. Personally, I don't give a shit what goes on here, but you got a minor in here. That is breaking the law."

"Minor?" He shook his head. "We take special care to…"

"Well, I guess it wasn't special enough. The boy is about sixteen, five ten, thin, blond, blue eyes. His name is Phillip Reynard. You help me to find him, get him back to his home, and we'll call it a day, okay?"

"No charges? No fine?"

"Not if I find him fast. I'll take a look around, alert your staff and we'll see if we can hunt him down. How many rooms you got going here?"

"There are three, excluding the main room. One is for light BSDM, one heavy—that's called the dungeon—and then there's the Stud room."

Sundar raised an eyebrow.

"Ah, it's in the dark, you walk in and, well…anything goes with anyone."

Sundar let out some air. "Okay, I'll ah…have a look around. I'm not going to be expected to…"

"Some people are here only to watch. But ah, Detective?" There was a faint smile on his face.

"Yeah?"

"That said, I would be careful if I were you. A guy who looks as good as you do, you're like deep rich chocolate for the chocoholic."

"I can take care of myself," Sundar snapped, not overly thrilled about being referred to as a piece of chocolate. "Thanks for the love."

Houser was laughing as Sundar left his office, but his forehead was damp with perspiration.

Sundar was cursing Joyce's name as he tentatively made his way down the long dingy corridor. He met several men on the way, all of whom looked like they'd visited paradise and hadn't quite returned to earth. Every single one propositioned him, offering to take him where they'd just been. He ignored them and walked on. The first door he came to was marked "Dungeon." Outside stood a man completely decked out in leather, including his head. He looked at him with chilly dark eyes and handed him a sheet of paper which contained a disclaimer as long as his arm.

Sundar glanced at the paper then back at the leather guy. "Ah, I'm looking for someone."

"Maybe you've found him."

"I...ah...inside, is there anyone who might have seemed really young, like..."

"Ah, you like tender flesh eh? You're a master, not a slave. I can tell."

"I'm a cop," he said.

"We have lots who like to play cop."

"I don't play cop, I am a cop."

He laughed. "You're fucking gorgeous is what you are. Go in, change your life. You'll never be the same."

There were some freaky sounding moans and groans coming out of that room. There was no shitting way he was going in there. "I think I'll pass. How many men are in there right now?"

"Three."

"Anyone who might look like they're under twenty?"

"Nope."

"Did your boss..."

"Yeah, he told us to cooperate. My balls are tightening thinking about that. Baby, you want to dominate me?"

"No thanks. And ah...aren't you the one who...?"

"Sure, but we can all use a change. I'd kill to see you naked."

"Don't do that." He smirked. "I'd have to arrest you."

"Naked?"

Sundar shook his head. "No," he said and walked on. The second door was open. He didn't hear any screams thankfully; just some very satisfied moans and groans. A young man stood outside the door, blond but not his sixteen year old. This one obviously worked here. He was dressed only in a G-string, his chest spattered with glitter. "This might be my lucky night. My horoscope said I was going to meet tall, dark, and sensational. Honey, you are hot."

"Try tall, dark and cop."

"Ah, the boss told us you'd be coming 'round. Looking for a kid, eh?"

"Anyone in that room meeting that description?"

"Why don't you go in and have a look around?" he invited, letting his tongue move slowly over his lips. "Bet you taste like ice cream."

"Chocolate actually," he said and brushed past him. There was some kind of a show going on. Several men sat around on overstuffed couches doing some kind of participant observation. They didn't notice his intrusion.

Sundar tried to keep his mind on the description of the boy but it wasn't so easy to make out the faces of the men in the room. The room was dimly lit and he'd counted and double counted seven audience members, if you could call them that, and two men up front who were providing the ah…stimulus. Sundar moved a little farther into the room and positioned himself in the corner. He found it hard to breathe all of a sudden. The room was warm and smelt of sex and sweat. The sounds vibrated around the rooms, moans and groans and grunts. He felt his cock harden. Swallowing hard, he kept his gaze on the two men at the front. One of them had been tied naked to the table, his arms over his head, his legs spread eagle and hoisted over his head. There was a cock ring around his shaft, a large object shoved into his anus, and some wicked looking clamps on his nipples. His aggressor moved around to the head of the table where the submissive one's head hung down, and lowered his erection into his mouth. "Suck it, you whore," he growled, as his cock disappeared deeper into his throat inch by inch. "Open your throat, deep throat me, slut, or I'll never let you come."

The sounds in the room grew more intense. Sundar unconsciously licked his lips as another man came up front and took off the sub's cock ring. His cock began to shoot reams of cum and the other man moved off the man's mouth and shot his own load, stroking his cock as he let his head go back.

It was the most erotic thing Sundar had seen in a long time. Not since that time in the locker room when Mark Sanborn had jacked off for him in the shower room. *Come on, Sun, let's see who takes the longest to shoot.* They'd been naked in the shower, Mark had soaped his entire body and then slowly, oh so slowly, began to stroke his own cock. Sundar'd been so hard, he'd almost lost it right there. He'd wanted to touch him but he couldn't. He'd wanted to put his cock in his mouth and taste him, but all he could do was stand there, suffering, watching as streams of cum floated between Mark's fingers. *You're not a faggot, are you, Sunny? Come on, jack off for me. I want to see how long it takes.* It had taken no time at all. He'd turned into the wall and grunted out his release.

Want to fuck me?

His eyes snapped open. He hadn't even realised they'd closed. He was staring into the bluest eyes he'd ever seen. "What?"

"Fuck me. Want to?"

"Ah, no," he said, shaking his head, his eyes finally taking in the slight build, the blond hair, the young baby face. "Actually," he straightened up to his full height, "you need to come with me."

Xander would have gone just about anywhere with him. He was one damn hot looking man. He had shoulder length silky black hair and huge velvety brown eyes. He was tall, big, and muscular, just the type of man he'd fantasised about, nothing he'd ever seen in Cary. He'd spotted him standing over in the corner all alone just as he was putting his clothes back on. He knew he had to have some of that. That would make his birthday! "Sure, baby. Where we going?"

"Home," the man said, taking him by the arm.

"Hey, ah, there's no need to drag me. I'm all yours, but I should tell the guy I came with that I'm leaving. It's not like he's my boyfriend or anything but…" Xander went to pull away but the other man held him fast.

"You're too young for that kind of boyfriend."

Xander gave him a strange look. "I am?"

"Yes, and you're in enough trouble already."

"Oh, not nearly enough trouble where you're concerned, baby." He gave him the once over and licked his lips. "You can spank me if I've been such a naughty boy."

"Stop that."

Xander suddenly found that he was halfway down the hall. He laughed and tried to pull out of his grip. "Where are we going again?"

"I'm taking you home. What in hell are you doing in a place like this anyway?"

"I could ask you the same thing, sweetheart."

"I was looking for you."

Xander narrowed his eyes. He was almost to the exit. "That's the most romantic thing I've ever heard."

"Romantic?"

"Oh yeah, it's right out of one of those sappy romance novels. You can tie to me to the bed when you get me home. I'm not going anywhere so you can, ah...loosen up. I like dominant men but you're carrying the act a little too far here, handsome. Really, I'm coming willingly."

The man stopped, eyed him. "This isn't a game. Your father is worried."

"My what?"

"Don't play games with me, Phillip."

Xander laughed. "That severe look you got going on is a real turn on, baby, but who in the hell is Phillip?"

"Yeah right, and don't call me baby."

Xander moved closer. So what if the man was a little nuts. He was really, really hot. "Forget about this Phillip guy, okay? Whatever he does for you, I can do better. I don't mind role play in bed, but I do insist that you call me by my name."

For a moment, their eyes met, and the other man seemed to freeze. He mouthed the word 'what?'

"Never mind. What's your name, stud?" Xander asked him softly.

"I'm not a...my name is Sundar Kingfisher, and I'm a cop." He took a step back which caused him to bump into the wall.

"Well, Sundar Kingfisher," Xander smiled and reached out to steady him, "I'm your prisoner. Take me where you want to. Handcuff me if you like. Just don't call me Phillip."

"Don't give me any trouble until I get you home. I'm officially off duty."

"You know, officer…"

"Detective."

"Detective," Xander trailed his gaze over the length of him, "you are a very pretty boy but you don't look very happy right now. In fact, maybe your visit here showed you what you've been missing in your life, and in your bed." Xander placed his hands on his hips. "Tonight was not an accident. Do you believe in karma?"

"I believe in sleep. Come on, let's go. Don't go playing shrink with me, kid." He took his arm again and pulled him towards the exit.

"I do work in a drug store."

"Well, stick to lipstick and cold remedies."

"How often do you have sex?"

"Ever heard the expression… that would be none of your business?"

"Yeah," he smirked, "but I don't pay much attention to that kind of thing. If I'm going to see you naked, I might as well get to know you."

"You're not going to see me naked," he snapped. "You're going home."

"So, what kind of name is Sundar, anyway? It sounds Latin." Xander glanced over at the manager suddenly. "Can you tell David I found a ride?" he called out.

Houser nodded at him. The coat check person passed him his coat at they got to the door.

"It's not Latin," Sundar muttered, glancing at the exchange as Xander reached out for his coat. "It's Tsalagi. You must come here all the time."

"Every weekend," he said. "You don't look Native."

"Every weekend? Jesus."

"I like it, so sue me, Tsalagi."

"Do you even know what Tsalagi is?"

"Sure, it's Cherokee to the pale faces. You look more Irish, dash of Italian maybe."

"I look like my mother."

"She must be a knock out."

Sundar sighed, grabbed his arm again and brushed past the doorman. He paused and looked at him. "Check ID from now on. If I hear of any other minors in here, I'll shut you down."

"Minors?" Xander croaked.

"I'll miss you," the doorman cooed, blowing him a kiss.

"Adopt a kitten," Sundar replied and, still holding Xander by the coat sleeve, climbed the stairs to the street. "Thank God," he said once they got out in the fresh air. "Come on, my car's across the street."

"What, no cruiser?" Xander teased.

Sundar unlocked the passenger side. "Get in, and no lip."

Xander grinned and opened the door. A few seconds later, Sundar Kingfisher was behind the wheel.

"Cool car."

He didn't reply.

"Do I get brownie points for knowing what Tsalagi is?"

"No."

"How about brownie points for knowing how hard your cock was in that room back there?"

That was met with an extremely hostile look.

"Whoops," Xander said. "You don't have much of a sense of humour, do you?"

The car roared to the stop sign and then took the corner on two wheels. Xander grabbed the dashboard. "If you fuck like you drive, I'm in for quite a night."

"Listen." He glared at Xander. "I am not going to fuck you. Stop saying that. I'm taking you home to your father."

"Ah, Sundar, listen…" he began. It was fun in the beginning but maybe he'd let it go on a bit too long. He needed to make it clear that he had the wrong guy.

"I said, not another word."

"O…kay."

They rode on in silence. Xander wondered how he was going to get back to Cary tonight after all this. By the time he got back to the club, David would be gone or hooked up for the night. Shit. Sometimes his impetuous nature landed him in big shit but when he looked at this guy — even if he was not really what one would call Mr. Personality — well, his heart sang, and his cock got hard, and…damn it, Sundar. *I think it might be love at first sight or some other impossible shit that I didn't believe in. Most likely, I just want this hunk to fuck me, get it out of my system. Not love. No.* Anyway given the fact Sundar was going to be even more pissed when he found out that he wasn't this Phillip guy, even that was a long shot.

When Sundar started checking addresses on a residential street, Xander started to get nervous.

"Okay, just tell me which house," Sundar grumbled. "I'm really tired now. Which one is it?"

"Honestly, I don't know."

"You don't know where you live? What are you, a moron?"

"Sundar, I don't live here. I live in Cary. I'm not this…"

"Here it is," he said, pulling up to the kerb and checking his piece of rumpled paper. "Get out. You can explain this to your father."

Xander sighed.

Sundar came around and opened the door.

"Listen, I don't live here. I'm not this Phillip guy. I'll show you my ID if you like."

"Yeah right, a fake one. Come on, get out."

"Okay," he sighed.

Sundar propelled the young man in front of him up the few steps to the porch of the small stone house. He rang the bell and waited, his hands clamped firmly on his shoulders.

Finally, a sleepy, disgruntled man wrenched the door open.

"Yeah?" he squinted.

"Mr. Reynard?"

"Yeah?"

"I'm Detective Kingfisher," Sundar flashed his badge. "I have your son."

The man stared at the young man in front of him. "This isn't my son. My son came home two hours ago. Didn't you get the message?"

"What do you mean, this isn't your son?" Sundar demanded.

"Don't you think I know my own son?"

"But he…"

"Look, I want to go to sleep. My son is home, and he's enough to handle. I don't need another one." The door slammed shut.

Sundar took his hands off the figure in front of him. "Who in the fuck are you?"

"I tried to tell you. You wouldn't listen."

"Jesus Christ!" Sundar exclaimed, marching down the stairs. "You think this is a game?"

"No," he said, shaking his head. "At first, it was fun but…"

Sundar wrenched open his car door.

"Hey, don't think you're leaving me here."

Sundar looked at him over the top of his car. "That's exactly what I'm doing."

"I have no place to go. You made me miss my ride. Give me a place to sleep tonight at least."

"Oh no." He opened the door and almost got in then he pointed at him. He was so angry, he was shaking. "You're lucky I don't arrest your ass!"

"Why? You're the one who didn't even check to see if I was the right guy."

"You let me believe you were."

"No, I didn't. I tried to tell you a few times."

"Bullshit!"

"Come on, Sundar, I'm sorry okay? Just let me bunk on your sofa tonight and then you never have to see me again. I'll grab the bus back tomorrow. Come on, I'm stuck."

"You should have thought of that before."

"I thought you were picking me up. I thought we were going to be together and damn it," he threw up his hands, "it's my birthday."

Sundar blinked. "Another load of bull?"

"Look." He took out his wallet and walked around to the driver's side. He handed him his social insurance card. "See?"

Sundar glanced at it. "Twenty-one? You look like a teenager."

He nodded with a smile. "I've always looked young for my age. Makes me a hit with the old queens."

"Ah, spare me." Sundar made a face. He hesitated. This was completely against his better judgement, taking some strange man home, but he couldn't leave him stranded. "Okay, get in."

"Perfect, yeah. Okay, so you're going to take me home and ravish me after all?" he laughed.

"None of that. Behave yourself, and no reading anything into it, okay?"

Xander slid into the passenger side of the car. "That won't be easy."

They fell into silence again and Sundar drove towards home. How could he have been so sloppy? This wasn't the kind of thing which had earned him his gold shield. He'd been distracted, tired maybe. He glanced at the young man sitting beside him. He acted like he didn't have a care in the world, and he'd made it clear that he was his for the taking. But, he couldn't. He wasn't like that. Sure, he'd lusted after a few football players when he was on the team, but that was adolescent stuff. He had sex with women, and one day, he'd find the right one.

"Get anything good on that radio?" he asked suddenly, reaching over and switching it on.

Sundar switched it off.

"Guess not. Are you always so grumpy?"

"Yes." His cell phone rang. He reached in his jacket pocket and opened it. It was Joyce.

"Hey, did you get your man...boy?" she laughed. "I tried to call you but you weren't picking up. The father called and..."

Sundar cast a look at Xander. "I know."

"Coming for breakfast?"

"Ah, I can't. I mean I'd like to but I'm really tired."

"I'll give you a massage."

"Sounds great but ah...another time, okay? Goodnight, Joyce." He closed the phone.

"Joyce?" Xander echoed. "You're fucking a guy called Joyce?"

Sundar shot him a look. "I'm not fucking…and it's none of your business."

"Yeah, you said that. Just a funny name for a guy."

"Why would you think I was fucking a guy?"

"Because you were hard as rock…"

"Okay, enough." He slammed on the brakes. He was now ready to strangle Xander. "Here's the deal. You keep your opinions about who you think that I'm fucking to yourself or you sleep outside."

"I won't say another word."

"I find that really hard to believe." He pulled his foot off the brake and put it on the gas. "Have you always had a tendency to say exactly whatever comes to your mind?"

"Yes actually."

"It's a bad habit."

"So is pretending to be someone that you're not." Sundar gave him a threatening look.

Xander put up his hands. "Okay, okay, sorry. Not another word, really. Sorry," he mouthed.

Luckily he did stay quiet until Sundar drove into his garage. He got out and used his remote to close the garage door. "Come on," he said to Xander. "I'll make up the sofa."

He could feel Xander standing close behind him as he put the key in his lock. He walked in, threw his keys on the kitchen counter and noticed that his answering machine was flashing.

"This is nice," Xander said as Sundar turned on the lamp in the living room. "Is it yours?"

"It's the bank's," he said.

"Yeah, but it's your house, right?"

"Yes."

"How many bedrooms?"

"Just one but I'm going to build a room downstairs when I get some time off. I'll get you some blankets and a pillow."

Xander sunk down onto the living room sofa. It was comfortable but Sundar's bed would have been far more inviting. He stood up again and walked around the living room. There was a large screen television set and a coffee table. On the mantle of the brick fireplace were some pictures. He picked one up and studied it. It was Sundar in uniform. There was another one, an older couple standing with a horse. "Your parents?" he asked as Sundar reappeared with the bedding.

"Yes. Put it down."

"You're not really expecting me to sleep on the sofa, are you?" Xander asked him, placing the photo carefully back in its place.

Sundar threw the blankets on the sofa. "What's wrong with it?"

"Nothing. It's just that..." He smiled. "You really think you're straight, don't you?"

"Look, I know who I am, okay? You're you, and I'm me and this here," he moved his hand back and forth, "isn't going to happen."

"Okay," Xander replied. "So what do I do with my feelings?"

"Introduce them to your hand."

Xander laughed out loud. "You're funny."

"Glad you think so," he replied. "Goodnight."

"Oh," Xander said, "your messages. Might be that Joyce guy...girl..."

"Well, the cross dresser will just have to wait until morning."

Xander grinned. "Night," he said as Sundar disappeared into the bedroom.

"And don't steal anything," he called out before he closed the door.

"Better lock your door," Xander called out, chuckling. He didn't get an answer. He looked sadly at the sofa. *Just my luck. The man of my dreams and he's Polly Anna's twin brother.* Oh well, he thought, stripping off his clothes. It wasn't exactly what he'd imagined for his twenty-first birthday, but at least he wasn't sleeping outside.

Chapter Two

Sundar was surprised to see that Xander guy sitting at his kitchen table when he came out of his room. He ran a hand through his tousled dark hair. He'd taken care to pull on some sweat pants and a t-shirt before he came out. It was almost noon and there he was, sitting at the table, his hair damp from a shower, sipping *his* coffee. "Oh hi," Xander said, raising the coffee cup. He looked a little guilty about something.

Sundar narrowed his eyes. "What did you do?"

"I made coffee. Want some?" His voice was overly bright.

"No, no, you did something. I'm a cop. I know guilty. Why do you look so sheepish?"

Xander pointed to the answering machine. The light was off. "I'm sorry."

Sundar stared at his answering machine. "You listened to my messages?"

"If you get angry that easy, Sundar, you're going to have high blood pressure and native people…"

"Don't. You listened to my messages!"

"I didn't mean to. It was an accident." He winced, standing up. "I called my boss, sister-in-law actually — nicknamed Attila — and told her I'd be late, and then the bus, well I called but there is no bus until tonight because I missed the early one, and I was wondering…see I—" He paused. "You hate me, right?"

"Can you at least tell me what the messages were? Did you erase them?"

"No. Well, maybe one of them. They weren't important. Your mother called, she said that, let's see…Mona's niece is in town and it would be nice if you asked her out. Does she have problems getting dates?"

"Who?"

"Mona's niece?'

"How in the hell should I know?"

"Oh yeah, and Joyce called. It's definitely a she and horny. She said she can't stop thinking about the last time and that, ah…you fuck like a champion." He beamed at him. "I, ah…didn't listen to the rest. It got kind of racy and personal."

Sundar swore under his breath. "That's it?" He raised an eyebrow.

"Yes."

"Did you happen to read my mail too?"

"No, didn't get to that yet."

Sundar walked over to pour himself some coffee. "I have to go to work at three. I'll drive you to Cary."

"Really?"

"Yep."

"Just 'cause you desperately want to get rid of me, right?"

He took a sip of coffee. "You think?" He gave him a look.

That damn guy grinned at him. Shit. He was like no one he'd ever seen. He looked like a God damned angel but he had a mouth like a...

"You have some great smelling shower gel."

"So glad you liked it."

"Do you like my coffee?"

"Not bad." He leaned against the counter and glanced out the window. The wind was blowing. It was going to be a chilly day.

"Sundar?"

"Um?" It felt weird to be called by his full name.

"Do you love this Joyce?"

He looked at him.

"I know, none of my business, right? It's just that she really seems hung up on you. You don't want to break her heart, do you?"

He blinked. "Where did you say you worked again?"

"Don't get smart. I'm serious."

"I don't think you know me well enough to be..."

"I'd like to." He moved closer. "I'd like to know you a hell of a lot better. Your hand is shaking."

"Shit," Sundar said, looking down to see that he'd slopped coffee all over himself.

"Let me," Xander said, getting a cloth from the sink. He began to wipe at his t-shirt and then moved the cloth down to his sweat pants where he wiped at the coffee spots a few times.

Sundar brushed his hand away. "Enough." His cock was reacting quite vigorously and it was becoming obvious.

Xander stopped his gaze on the bulge in Sundar's sweats. He licked his lips. "You're fully loaded."

Sundar put down the coffee cup. He looked embarrassed. "I wake up like this in the morning. Nothing there."

"I can fix it." He reached out his hand.

Sundar pushed it away. "It's okay. It will pass."

"Why do you want it to pass when I can fix it?" Xander suddenly felt his desire as if a tidal wave had taken hold of him. He wanted him. He wanted him more than any man he'd ever seen. "Please." He met Sundar's gaze and saw him swallow hard.

"It's not…" Sundar began but his voice faltered.

Xander reached out again. He gripped the top of Sundar's grey sweat pants. This time Sundar didn't prevent him. Xander pulled and they fell down around his ankles. Sundar looked away but he didn't move. "You're beautiful," Xander said. "You have a beautiful cock."

Sundar reached back with his hands and gripped the counter top. Xander slid to his knees and ran his hands up alongside of Sundar's thighs. He licked the head of Sundar's cock. He heard Sundar suck in some air. "Relax," he said. "It's okay. Just relax."

Sundar closed his eyes. He wasn't sure what the hell he was doing and why, but when Xander's lips closed around his shaft, he lost of all sense of reality. He was back in that locker room with Mark, who was showing off his body, taunting him. Only this time, Mark was touching him. "Oh God," he managed. His cock was pulsing now in Xander's throat. Deeper, deeper, this guy was swallowing him whole. "Oh shittt…shittttt!" He let his head go back and his cock pumped out its release while a hand lovingly stroked it to completion.

When he finally came down to earth, he looked down to see that angelic face looking up at him, his lips moist, and his gaze filled with need. Sundar touched his cheek. "I'm sorry."

"For what?"

"I came so fast, I…"

"According to Joyce, it's not normal. You can go all night." He smirked.

Sundar clicked his tongue. "Never mind. Look that was great. I mean, you're really talented."

"Thanks…but…?"

"I'm not…I mean, I'm straight."

"Give me a night to prove you wrong?" Xander stood up, met his eyes.

"No, I mean…"

"Sundar, try it once. You want to, don't you? You're curious, at least admit that. Curiosity doesn't make you gay."

"Okay, I'm curious. I think…" he took a breath, reached down and pulled up his sweatpants, "I think it has to do with something that happened back in high school." He put some distance between them. "I've never told anyone this. I don't why I'm telling you."

"What happened?"

"It was this guy on the football team. He used to like to jerk off in front of me."

"You played football?"

"Almost made it to the big leagues but I banged up my knee."

"Shit."

He shrugged. "Anyway, maybe that's why. Maybe I never carried it out and I should have, got it out of my system, you know?"

"Sundar." Xander came closer again.

Sundar felt his heart beat speed up a bit.

"Sexual orientation is not something you get out of your system. Is it good with women?"

"It's okay."

"Just okay? Joyce says you were fantastic. But you don't feel that with her, do you?"

"No."

"I'm going to be honest with you, and I want you to be honest with me, okay?"

"I'll try." He wasn't good with these kinds of things.

"You better. I just had your cock in my mouth," he joked.

He felt stricken. "You won't tell anyone that, will you?"

"No. But listen, back at The Cave, I saw raw desire on your face in that room, and I imagined that you were looking at me like that. You're the man of my dreams, Sundar. Give me a chance to rock your world and win your heart."

Sundar cleared his throat. "Xander." He wasn't sure what to say to that. There was something, some chemistry between them, and he'd felt it too.

"Give me one night, one night, baby. And if it's not what you want, I'll walk away. We never have to speak about it again. But if you don't try it, you'll have to live with this feeling of uncertainty for the rest of your life."

"I need to get dressed if I'm going to drive you home," he said, rinsing his cup in the sink. It almost slipped out of his hand a few times. He put it aside and left the kitchen.

When he got to his room, he sunk down onto the bed. He'd hardly slept at all last night with Xander on the sofa. He had images of him lying there beside him naked and it drove him half mad with desire. He couldn't believe he'd let this complete stranger suck his cock. But damn it, it had been so good, even if he'd come too fast, and it had only lasted a few minutes. He had to get a handle on this stuff. He wasn't the type of man to lose control. He wasn't going to put everything he'd worked so hard for in jeopardy for one night of debauchery.

He pulled on some clothes and tried to think of what he was going to say. He'd shower later at the police station, after he dropped this guy off home where he belonged.

When he came back out, Xander was sitting on the sofa. He glanced up at him. "You're going to drive me home, aren't you?"

"That's what you wanted, didn't you?"

"Yes, I mean, no," he sounded frustrated. "I can call my sister-in-law, tell her I'm taking a few days off."

He sighed. "I don't think it's a good idea."

"What's it going to hurt? What are you worried about, Sundar? Is it that someone will find out, or you will? It's just sex after all. We won't do anything you don't want to."

"And this is so damn important to you?"

"Yes," he said, "because I think you might be the one, and I'm not about to let you slip away without a fight."

There were tears in his eyes.

Sundar sighed. "You're insane."

"You feel it too. You feel something when you look at me. Even if it's just desire, I know it's there. Tell me it's not and we'll leave now."

He sighed. "No, it's there," he said. There was no use in lying.

"Last night, I hardly slept." Xander met his gaze.

He nodded. "Me neither."

Xander smiled. "I'll call my sister-in-law, tell her I won't be coming in to work." He hoped she could find another babysitter. "What time will you be back tonight?"

"A little after midnight," he said hesitantly. "And, Xander, if I decide when I come back that this has all been a mistake, and that I don't want to go through with it, then—"

"The sofa is still here. I'll sleep on it another night and take the bus out first thing in the morning. I even have cab fare."

"Okay. Fair enough. I've got some errands to do, so... Help yourself to what's in the fridge."

"Sundar? Wait." He reached out and took his arm. He pulled him closer and then reached up and placed a hand behind his head. He brought his mouth down on his and kissed him softly on the mouth.

The kiss lingered on Sundar's lips, leaving him warm all over. He smiled faintly. "I got to go."

* * * *

"You're going to get burned," David told him on the phone a few hours later. "Closet cases are always closet cases. They may slip in and out but they always return to their dark holes. I have some rather painful former experience with that."

David with a painful past relationship—Xander would have never figured that. He regretted calling him now because what David had to say was the last thing he wanted to hear, even if it was true. "He's not in the closet, technically," Xander finally managed to say rather unconvincingly.

"Oh, they have a new name for it now, do they?" The way David laughed grated on him.

Xander fell silent. He wanted to tell David about the unusual way they'd met, and how they were complete opposites. He wanted to confess that this impossible desire burning inside him for a man he hardly knew, wouldn't allow him to just walk away. *If I leave, I'll never see him again.*

"Why don't you let me drive down there now and pick you up?"

"No, it's okay. I'll see you tomorrow."

"What about your bitch sister-in-law?"

"David," he said, "can't you just call her my boss?"

"Okay, okay, your boss then. What did she say when you called and said…"

"She was pissed off because I had promised to stay with the baby tonight, but in the end she told me to take the week off. I think she's glad to get rid of me for awhile so that she can have Nathan all to herself. I can't blame her. But I do have to get back Thursday. I have my night course."

"You're going to stay there with that strange closet case until Thursday? What if it doesn't work out?"

"Look, I do have to find a work placement for after the holidays. Maybe I could check out apartments here too at the same time."

"You can't afford it."

"I'll find a job here part time."

"You need to think things through, Xander."

"And what's made you into Mr. Practical all of a sudden?"

"Xander, I know our relationship is just sex but I'd like to think we're friends, and lately…look, I can find a job there too in Raleigh. We can share a place, and I'll help you out until…"

"No. I mean, I want to make my own way. Thanks, anyway David. And we are friends."

"I'll pick you up Thursday. Call me."

"Thanks." Xander hung up. Did he know what in hell he was doing? Not really, but somehow he didn't seem to have a choice.

* * * *

"Did you get any sleep last night, Sunny?"

Sundar had been staring at the same report for the last ten minutes. He glanced up suddenly to see Joyce standing in front of his desk. "Ah, not much."

"I'm sorry about sending you on a wild goose chase last night. Reynard called by the way, said you brought the wrong kid to his door. What's up with that?"

He sighed. *Fucker had to call.* "I was tired, and this…not a kid, a young man. He ah…looks young and he didn't tell me he wasn't Phillip Reynard. It's a long, stupid story."

"Why wouldn't he tell you? He likes getting arrested?"

She was looking at him intensely, wanting an answer.

"Look, Joyce, this fraud case has me a little baffled and I'm getting some pressure from upstairs to wrap it up. The facts aren't fitting together like some of the others on the taskforce seem to want to believe. I was a little preoccupied. Let's forget it, okay? Reynard needs to pay more attention to the activities of his son."

"Agreed. Look, how about a late supper tonight? I notice you haven't taken a break and it's after seven. I have some leftovers at my place and…"

"I can't. Sorry. Not tonight." He lowered his head back to the report, hoping she'd go away. She started to say something else when someone called to her to say she had a phone call. Sundar breathed a sigh of relief when she walked off. Xander had been right about one thing. It wasn't fair to lead her on when he really had no romantic interest in her.

He stared at the phone. He almost picked it up several times to tell Xander that he should really take that bus home to Cary tonight. He'd called the terminal — it left at eight. Xander would only have twenty minutes now to make it. It was too late. He'd have to sleep on the sofa and go home tomorrow.

Sundar ran a hand through his hair. What in hell had he been thinking, taking a stranger into his house, and leaving him there unsupervised? He could be a thief, a maniac. He could be anyone, even if he did have a great ass and…

He sighed deeply. Yes, he'd noticed. Those faded jeans he wore did a great job of showing off those hard round globes, and profiling the bulge which lay behind the zipper. And those blue eyes. He'd never seen eyes so blue before, the colour of cornflowers, or periwinkles. There, he was losing it now, wasting his time contemplating the exact shade of a man's eyes. *But his mouth, his mouth was something else, skilful and soft and…* He was sweating, and his cock was jutting uncomfortably against the zipper of his black pants.

"Are you okay, Sun?" Darrel Patton, another detective on the task force suddenly perched himself on the edge of Sundar's desk.

Sundar wiped the sweat off his forehead, shifted a bit in his seat. "Yeah, sure. Why?"

"You look like you're coming down with something?"

Coming down with something? Maybe he was.

* * * *

Xander almost jumped out of his skin when he heard someone walk in the front door. He'd been snooping in Sundar's closet, looking at his shirts, his pants, inhaling the scent of him. It was a guilty pleasure, and he'd been bored, watching the clock until he knew Sundar would be back.

He checked the clock now. It was barely nine o'clock, too early for Sundar, unless... "Sundar?" he called out, hurrying out of the bedroom, "I thought…"

The woman who stood there looked as surprised to see him as he was to see her. She was a short little woman about forty five or so with auburn hair and dark brown eyes. She was very pretty and she gave him and uncertain smile. "Hello, I'm Sundar's mother." She looked down at the casserole dish she was holding. "I made his favourite—lasagne. I don't use the key very often," she giggled, looking a little guilty. "I'm not supposed to. He doesn't like that. But he hasn't been eating well lately, and…oh, I'm sorry," she said, "I haven't given you a chance to speak. You are?"

He held out his hand. "Xander, Xander Frey." He guessed they were both guilty of something.

"Sophie Macgregor-Kingfisher." She shook it. "I didn't know Sundar had a guest staying over. Did you play ball together?" She took the casserole over and placed it on the counter.

"No. Ah, it's a police matter. He's helping me find a place to live. I'm doing a work placement in the winter and I need an apartment."

"Oh. A work placement in what field?"

"Hotel management. I'd like to get in to one of the big hotels here in the city. They won't pay me much, if anything, so I need a cheap place to live."

"That's not easy to find," she said. "For how long do you need a place?"

"Three months."

"Um, most places will only rent for a year. We have a spare room. It's Sundar's old room but he doesn't need it. He just bought this little house. Cute, isn't it? But it needs a woman's touch."

"It needs something," Xander said. "Your son doesn't strike me as the decorator type."

Sophia laughed. "I made the curtains. He was going to just go with blinds. Anyway, I got away from what I was saying. If you decide you want the room, it's yours. It would be great having a young man in the house again. I've been a little lonely since Sundar left."

"I can understand that. That's very kind of you, Sophia."

She shrugged. "Well, guess I'll go. Can you tell him I dropped this off and get him to eat?"

"I will."

"Xander," she said, pausing on the way to the door.

"Yeah?"

"Do you know if there's someone? Is he dating?"

"Really, Mrs. Kingfisher, I..."

"Sophie."

"Sophie. I can't tell you that. We don't know each other very well yet."

"Do you have a sister?" She laughed.

"No."

She shrugged. "Remind him that he's taking out Mona's niece."

"I will."

"She went through a breakup with her boyfriend in New York. She could use a little pick me up. Tell Sun to take her someplace classy. And I'll give him the money."

He smiled. "Okay."

She lifted a hand and disappeared out the door.

His mother was sweet, but she was completely in the dark about her son.

* * * *

Sundar sat in his car outside for the longest time before getting out. There was a light burning in the living room and he could see the reflection from the television. Xander hadn't left. He hadn't taken the bus back to Cary. He was still there, and he was waiting.

When the key turned in the lock and he opened the door, Xander had come to stand in the kitchen. "Hi," he said.

"Hello." Sundar shrugged out of his jacket and threw his keys down on the counter.

"You look surprised to see me, or is it disappointment?"

Sundar cleared his throat. "I've been thinking about this all evening and…"

"Me too."

Xander looked a little breathless, his chest heaved slightly. He was definitely sporting a hard on.

Sundar's gaze settled on his crotch then returned to his face. "This... It's kind of ridiculous, don't you think?"

"Absolutely." He nodded. "But you are feeling it?"

Yeah, he was feeling it. His cock was feeling it too.

"I can just suck you off again if..."

Sundar closed the distance between them. "No, I don't want you to just suck me off," he grunted, yanking him up against him with a force that surprised both of them. "I want to do everything with you, everything, and God, I want to fuck you. I want to fuck that beautiful ass of yours." He looked down at him. "Say yes," he pleaded, his heart pounding in his chest. "Tell me you'll let me."

"Yes," Xander moaned, "yes." He reached up and wound his arms around his neck, kissed him hard. "I want you."

That sent a tingle down Sundar's spine. Xander wanted him. He wanted his cock inside of him. Sundar didn't want to think about what that meant. He just wanted to touch him, taste him.

Clothes were falling to the floor, first his shirt, and then Xander's. The pants came next, Xander brushing his hands aside to take down his own pants. "If you do it, I'll come right here," he whispered. "Shit." He struggled with the zipper, practically ripping it apart.

Sundar walked to the bedroom, grabbing Xander's hand without looking at him and pulling him along. His other hand undid his own pants, and he stepped out of them as he got to the entrance of his room.

Xander stumbled over the pants, then placed a hand on Sundar's hard ass and slipped it down inside the dark blue briefs. "You have a great ass," Xander groaned, moving up against his back and running his hands down over his chest from behind and then pushing the briefs down over his erection and swallowing hard as they dropped to the floor.

Sundar leant back against him, breathing hard now as Xander fondled his cock and smoothed his hand over one of his ass cheeks. He felt him bite his shoulder gently, fingers curving around his shaft.

"You're trembling all over," Xander told him.

"You too."

The hand left his cock and travelled up to his chest, brushed over one nipple, tweaked it, went to the other. "You don't mind if I touch you for a few minutes?"

"You're driving me mad."

"That's the goal." He laughed softly. "God, you're a beautiful man. My heart is coming out of my chest. Feel how hard I am."

Sundar turned around in his arms. He stood back a little; let his gaze travel over the length of him. He was slender, his skin smooth and soft. His cock was a good size and so hard, it was dripping cum. "God," he whispered, letting his hand moved down over that smooth chest then examining his cock with his fingers almost in wonder.

Xander sucked in some breath and let his head go back. "Sundar, Christ."

Sundar met his gaze then bent his head to kiss his throat, his chest... As he continued downwards, he sunk to his knees. He rested his head against Xander's erection for a moment. Xander touched his hair. "It's okay, baby," he said.

He lifted Xander's cock in his hand as if it were suddenly fragile, his body aching, his cock pulsing. His lips went to the lip where he slowly licked the cum from around the head and then sucked the underside, moving his lips to his balls.

He was aware that Xander made a sound in his throat and felt his fingers tighten in Sundar's hair. He took his cock into his mouth, surprised at the taste, not unpleasant but rather salty. He took it deeper, tightening his lips, shielding his teeth, trying not to gag, but he'd heard that came with time.

Xander began to thrust his hips and Sundar glanced up at him, holding still. His eyes were still closed. He was somewhere in some pleasant place, and Sundar was suddenly addicted. He wanted to increase that pleasure, drive him crazy, made him come hard, so hard that his teeth would rattle and…

"Ahhh, yes!" Xander muttered and Sundar backed off as he tasted the cum in his mouth, choking a little as he reared back, licked his lips. Xander had turned to the wall, bent over, his hand on his cock. His body seemed to heave. When he turned around, he was smiling. "Shit. Are you sure you've never done that before?"

Sundar wiped his mouth on the back of his hand. He smiled and went down on the floor on his elbows. "Was it good?"

"Good?" He laughed and came down on the floor in front of him. "It was fucking great. Wow, you're a natural."

"A natural cock sucker, imagine that." He was meant to be a joke but it didn't sound like one.

Xander titled his head. "Second thoughts?"

Sundar ran his gaze over him again. "Oh no, no second thoughts. Do you have what we need?"

"Lube, condoms, yeah."

"Good." He got up off the floor. "Get them." He walked over to the bed and lay down.

Xander went out to the living room to get the lube and condoms. He always carried a little bottle and three or four safes in his jacket pocket, in case. As he held them in his hand, he paused. He could see Sundar though the door, lying naked on the big four poster bed. He swallowed. It wasn't that he didn't want him. Maybe he wanted him too damn much. And then what would happen after? It made no sense. He'd never agonised before intercourse before. He'd see a guy that turned him on, and boom, that was it. They'd fuck and move on. But this wasn't the same. He'd known it from the beginning. The risk to his heart was great this time. Would it be worth it?

"Xander?"

He heard his voice. *Yes. No matter what happened after, it would be worth it, all the pain, all the...*

"Xander?"

"Coming," he replied, walking back into the room. "Hi," he said, his voice sounding like a moan as he came to the side of the bed and looked down at him. His body, so muscular and toned, so...and that cock... "You must have won contests in high school," he grinned.

Sundar made room on the bed and Xander lay down beside him. Sundar took the lube and the condoms. He smoothed back Xander's hair. The way he was looking at him was making his pulse race. "I think I'm having a heart attack."

Sundar kissed his mouth softly. "Don't do that. Roll over."

Xander was shaking as he rolled onto his stomach. He was the one who suddenly felt like the virgin.

"Come up on your knees a little, spread your legs."

His voice was so damn sexy, deep, and smooth. Xander got up onto his knees, spread his legs.

"Hot, you're so hot, grab onto the headboard."

One greased finger went up inside of him and began to prod him. Xander licked his lips. One finger was suddenly replaced by two.

"I want to make sure you're ready for me. I want this to be good for you. I'm big."

"I want to take all of you up inside me. I can take it…ooh…Sundar, um, keep doing that." He was fucking him quite pleasantly with his fingers and Xander felt himself opening up completely to the invasion.

"Play with yourself," Sundar urged. "I want to watch while I do this, you mind?"

"Whatever you want," Xander said, moving his hips to the movement of Sundar's fingers and stroking his cock at the same time.

"Yeah, that's it," Sundar urged. "Um, beautiful, that's it, baby. Um.

You're doing it for me." He was lost, his mind filled with the beauty of the blond angel who was moving his body in a way which fuelled his desire like never before. He continued to work his fingers into him, loving the way his body was responding to his manoeuvers. His cock was near to exploding and he knew he'd have to take him soon, possess him with his arms, and his lips and his cock. "Xander," he moaned.

He withdrew his hand and moved in behind him, lowering his lips to Xander's shoulder, smelling his hair, feeling the softness of it on his cheek. "Xander," he hissed, pressing him down to all fours as he seized his hips and positioned his cock. He felt the air go out of him as his cock took control, plunging deep into Xander's ass.

He closed his eyes, his hips beginning to move and his mind went blank, a blissful white out of pleasure gripping him, coursing through his cock as his groin slapped against Xander's ass. Their bodies worked together, slick flesh sliding against each other.

Xander lifted his hips, matched his frenzied movements perfectly, his palms balancing on the mattress. "Sundar, Sundar, Jesus, Holy God…yes, yes…Babeeeeeeeeeeeeee!"

His cock began to empty like a faucet suddenly opened full force. He held onto to Xander's hips with full force and emptied his balls into him.

Xander was lying flat on his stomach, soaked with sweat, his face turned to the side. Sundar scrambled back from him and reclined on the bottom of the bed. Xander flipped over on his back. He closed his eyes, listened to his heart slam in this chest, and touched the stickiness of his dwindled erection. His eyes closed. If there had been any doubt, it was now dashed. He'd never experienced anything like it. He felt as if he'd had sex for the first time and all that people said about it, was true. It was incredible. It was earth shattering. And damn it, why couldn't Joyce do this for him, or some other woman? Why this young man with the angelic face and…

He was watching him quietly now, this angel, this demon who'd come to tempt him with heaven, and shatter his existence. How could he tell his parents what he was? How could he let his fellow officers on the police force know? He couldn't. No one must ever know. He couldn't get too attached to this guy. Xander could easily become an obsession. "So?" Xander smiled. "Are you all right?"

"Fine," he sat up.

Xander reached for him and he got up off the bed.

"Where are you going?"

"Nowhere, just to get a drink." He left the room. He had to suddenly. He stood in front of the open refrigerator and scoffed down half a pint of orange juice. He felt tears threaten and he swallowed them, his throat hurting. What in hell was the matter with him? He hadn't shed tears since he was seven. His father would have chastised him if he'd done that. He hung his head, only lifting it again when he heard Xander's voice from behind him.

Xander knew something wasn't right. After that kind of mind-blowing sex, usually your partner stayed in bed. You talked, you cuddled, and you made love again. You didn't walk out into the kitchen and stand naked in front of an open refrigerator.

"You want me to leave?" He held his breath, afraid of the answer.

Sundar closed the fridge and turned around. "No, that's okay. You can use the sofa."

Xander felt that in the pit of his gut. That hurt, really hurt. But he'd asked for it. *I think I love you.*

"I'll get the blankets and…"

"Sundar, Jesus Christ," he said, reaching out to him. "Can't we talk about this? Did I do something?"

He paused, looked at him. "No. Look," he sighed, "you asked for a night. I gave you a night. It was nice. It's over now. We need to get back to our lives."

"You mean, you need to get back to pretending you're straight. You're not straight, Sundar. No straight man fucks me the way you just did."

"I need to get the blankets," he said.

Xander sunk down on the edge of the sofa. He put his face in his hands. His friend Mike had once told him back in high school something back in high school that came to his mind now. *We'll all have our experience with the straight guy who likes to live dangerously. He'll probably be the one to break your heart. Those tough macho types always do.* Except Sundar wasn't straight. He could be bi, but he wasn't sure if he really believed that either. Whatever he was, he wasn't intending on being with him.

Xander looked up at him when he came back out with the blankets. He had put on a robe, and his expression was hard to read.

"What time is your bus?"

"At seven. Too early for you, you have to work the evening shift. I'll grab a cab."

"No. It's okay. I'm off tomorrow. I'll take you to the bus."

Xander met his eyes. "Don't do this, Sundar. We could be good together. We are good together. That was the best..."

"Don't," he put up a hand. "It was what it was. It was really nice. Thank you. But I can't." He shook his head.

"Can't what?"

"I can't be gay."

"But you are gay."

"Well," he uttered a faint laugh, "I'll have to live with that."

"But it will destroy you."

"No," he shook his head, "you could destroy me, Xander."

Xander flinched. He stood there frozen as Sundar mumbled goodnight and walked into his room. He shut the door behind him. Tears ran silently down Xander's face. *Okay. Here comes the pain.*

Chapter Three

When Sundar opened his eyes the next morning, he realised that Xander had left. Maybe it was for the best. Sundar had hardly slept. He checked the time every five minutes and listened to Xander pace the floor in the living room. He must have finally fallen asleep around five and when the alarm went off at six, he knew already that he'd left. And why shouldn't he have, after the way he'd treated him, like Xander had some contagious disease that he didn't want to catch.

He rolled over in bed, ran his hand over the place where Xander had knelt, where he fucked him. He closed his eyes, moaned. His hand went to his hard cock and he pictured Xander there, stroking his own cock as Sundar finger fucked his ass. His smile, his kiss, the desire in his eyes; was he supposed to just live without that? No. He'd have to have it now, now that he'd been inside another man, he knew he'd have to be inside another or go insane. Never the same man, that was the key of course, not to get too involved, fall in love. *Love.* He could love a woman, a woman that he had a lot in common with, have conversation with. And he could satisfy a woman in bed, he knew that. He'd get his own satisfaction with strangers, strangers who expected nothing. He could handle that. And Xander, well, Xander would find some nice gay man who could be with him, and fuck that gorgeous ass of his, and be the recipient of all that desire in his eyes. They were like periwinkles, his eyes. He knew that now.

* * * *

"Why didn't you call me? I would have come to get you."

"What are you doing here, David?" Xander was in no mood for a lecture.

"I came in for a prescription."

"Got the clap?"

"Funny man. No, try sinusitis. I thought you were taking the entire week off, going to look for an apartment in the city?"

"Didn't happen. I got in early so I told Barbara I'd work. I might as well."

David leaned on the counter. "What happened? You look sad."

Xander felt his eyes light with tears. "Nothing. Nothing happened. It's okay, alright?"

"I told you, men like that…"

"Look, that woman looks like she needs something on aisle six," he slipped out from behind the cash register. "See you later."

David walked off towards the back of the drug store to get his prescription and Xander went into the bathroom.

He closed the door and placed his head against the wall. He sobbed silently for a few minutes then dried his eyes and came back out.

Barbara was standing there. "Where've you been? There has been a customer waiting for help. I can't do everything. What's wrong with you? You got a cold? Why are your eyes all red?"

Xander sniffed, wiped at his eyes. "I, ah...nothing. Just allergies."

"Since when? Allergy season is over with."

"Barbara, please," he pleaded. "Just leave it alone."

She nodded. "Fine. Do your job." She marched off to the dispensary.

* * * *

The holidays came and Xander avoided going into Raleigh. He even turned down the opportunity to go with his brother on their annual shopping day, something he usually looked forward to each year.

He devoted himself to his studies and did well on his final exam. He'd decided to try and find a work placement in Cary, but it was two days to the deadline, and he'd found nothing.

"You should really check out some of the big hotels," Barbara said, stringing garland on the tree as he sat on the living room sofa, playing with his niece. "I thought that's what you wanted, to get out of this stifling little town."

He nodded. "I changed my mind."

Barbara put down the garland. "What happened back there?"

"Nothing."

"Xander, you've been down since you came back that time. Is it a man?"

"I don't want to…"

"I know you think I don't like you. That's not true. You're Nat's brother and he loves you. I only want the best for you. It hasn't been easy for you since your parents died and…"

"Thanks," he said, looking at her. "You've been kind to me, Barb. You didn't need to have me here, horning in on your life."

She shrugged. "If I can help you, use my influence in any way… Listen, I do know a woman, the wife of a pharmacist I went to school with. Her brother is the manager of a hotel in Raleigh, the Carolina Cove. Maybe I could get you a placement there."

"I'd have to have a place and…"

"We could help you out money wise."

"No." He thought of Sundar's mother. She had offered, but could he do that? Could he bear to see Sundar again? And Sundar probably would be really pissed off. Well, to hell with him. He didn't want him in his life, but he wouldn't stop him from making his own. "Okay," he said to his sister in-law, "see if you can get me a three month placement there. I know someone who offered me a room in the city. I'll try to find the number."

* * * *

He'd stopped short of asking her to marry him. And he hadn't really asked her to move in with him either. He wasn't quite sure how it had happened. He might have mentioned something about it being a good idea, the two of them…in the future, the possibility…since they had so much in common.

Now Joyce was calling the movers.

His head was spinning. In fact, it had been spinning for the last couple of weeks. It was for the best, wasn't it? They were both cops. They understood one another, the pressures of the job. And his mother was so excited.

"What should I get Joyce for Christmas?"

Sundar raised his head from his coffee cup and stared at her. "Nothing."

"What do you mean nothing? She's practically our daughter in-law, right Clint?" Sophie glanced over at his father, who sat on the other side of the table. He hadn't said a word, as usual.

"Liquor is always a good choice. Cops like to drink," Clint said, sipping his tea.

Sundar stood up. "Yes, we're all lushes."

"The ones on the reserve were."

Sundar ignored him. "Don't worry about it," he said to his mother. "Joyce doesn't expect you to buy her anything."

"What are you buying her?" his father looked at him.

Surprised by the question, he shrugged. "Perfume."

"Yep, that's what I expected," he muttered. "No imagination."

"But you buy mom perfume every damn year."

"Yes, because that's what she wants. That cop won't want that. You're going to share your life with this woman and you don't even know her."

"Do you have to find fault with every fucking decision I make?"

"From what I hear, you didn't have much say in it," he replied.

"Sundar, stop," his mother clucked her tongue, cutting him off before he could say something else. "And you too, Clint," she shot her husband a look. "Christmas is coming."

"And that's supposed to make a difference?" Clint laughed.

Sundar kissed his mother on the cheek. "Gotta go."

"You are coming for Christmas dinner?" His mother sounded panicked, following him to the door.

"I'll have to see what Joyce has planned. I'll be by, don't worry." He nodded at his father and left by the side door. He stepped outside, shivering a little. *Share my life with Joyce? Is that what I'm doing? I thought we were just shaking up.*

* * * *

Xander stared at the phone a long time before he dialled the number. It rang five times and he almost put it down. But just before he did, it picked up. It was a man, his voice sounding familiar. For a moment, his heart skipped a beat and he thought it was Sundar. When the voice said hello the second time, he realised that the man sounded older.

"Ah, hello, Mr. Kingfisher?"

"Yes."

"I'm calling for Sophie. Is she there?"

"Just a minute," he said.

Xander heard him call out her name. He'd thought hard about taking Sophie Kingfisher up on her invitation to rent a room at her house. On one hand, it was a great idea. He was sure it would end up being a lot cheaper than renting an apartment and he wouldn't have a lease. On the other hand, she was Sundar's mother, and chances were, Sundar would come to the house eventually to see his parents. Who in hell was he kidding? He wanted to see Sundar again, even if it killed him. And this was a surefire way to do it.

"Hello?" a woman's voice came onto the phone suddenly.

"Mrs. Kingfisher. I don't know if you remember me, Xander. We met at—"

"Of course I remember you. Did you like the lasagne?"

"Yeah, it was great. How are you?"

"Fine, fine. And yourself?"

"Could be better. Listen Mrs..."

"Sophie."

"Sophie, I was wondering if that room you offered is still for rent?"

"Of course. Did you find your work placement?"

"The Carolina Cove."

"Oh that's a lovely place and within walking distance."

"Great."

"When would you like to move in?"

"January third, is that okay?"

"That would be fine. I'm sure Sundar will be glad to see you again."

"No. I mean, listen Sophie, I'd appreciate if you didn't say anything about me taking the room just yet."

"Did you have a falling out?"

"Let's say we don't see eye to eye on a couple of things. I'm sure we can work it out though." He closed his eyes. If only that were true.

"Well, who I rent a room to has nothing to do with my son. Don't worry about it. He'll find out when he'll find out. Anyway, he might not even come for Christmas yet since he and Joyce are moving in together."

Xander gripped the phone.

"Are you still there?"

"Yeah. Him and…Joyce, the cop, they're moving in together?"

"Looks like it. And maybe now he'll go to her folks for Christmas. I don't think she's from here originally."

Xander didn't realise that he'd stopped listening. He was picturing Sundar in his head, his thick black hair, all those delectable muscles, his cock and the way it had felt inside of him. God, how they'd fucked that night. Sundar had filled him with pleasure, in a way he'd never known. Now, all he felt was empty. *I'm pretty sure that I love your son, Sophie. I love him so much.*

"…Texas. You know what I mean?"

"Texas. She's from Texas?" He snapped back to reality.

"Who?"

"Joyce," he almost choked on her name.

"Why yes, but what I said was I think my sister may be coming from Texas."

"Oh, that's nice."

"So, don't you worry about money, Xander, you pay what you can, when you can. You hear me?"

"Ah no, Sophie, you tell me how much and…"

"We'll haggle when you get here. I'm so excited. I'm going to cook up a storm."

He laughed. "Okay, thanks again. I appreciate this."

"You have yourself a nice Christmas now, you and your folks."

"We will," he said and hung up.

David couldn't stop staring at him. "I don't believe you," he said for the twentieth time. "I fucking don't believe you. I am now convinced — you're nuts."

Xander folded his arms across his chest. "Listen, I agreed to go to The Cave, don't push it. There are only so many times you can insult me before I get pissed off, David."

"Xander, think about it. This man treats you like shit and you..."

"He didn't treat me like shit. He never promised me anything. We had sex, he decided that he's straight and that's it."

"He's a liar, and now he's shaking up with a woman?"

"It doesn't matter what he does, it's over—if there was ever anything between us to begin with."

"You're right," David stopped at a red light, "it is over. It's over for him, but not you. What do you do? You rent a room from the guy's mother! Do you like slamming your head against a concrete wall?"

He sighed. David was right. "Okay, fine. I want to see him again. In fact, I want him okay? I want him even if I'm only going to be his dirty little secret. I figure he'll want me too." Tears rolled down his face.

David pulled the car off to the side of the road. "I'm sorry," he said. "You're really hung up on this guy."

He nodded.

"Do what you need to, Xander. I won't judge you. I just don't want you to get hurt."

"Oh, it's way too late for that. Look, I saw him that night and I knew I had to have him. And after we were together, I knew my instinct to stick with him that night had been right even if I kind of tricked him into it by pretending to be someone else. There was a spark between us, and after awhile, he felt it too. He just can't accept it. So..."

"Wouldn't it be better to just try to get over him?"

"I tried that. I figured after a few days, a month, I wouldn't think about him anymore, but he's still the first thing on my mind in the morning and the last thing on my mind before I go to bed at night. If I have to be his slut, I will be. I'll hang onto the hope that one day he'll be able to accept who he is, until he sends me away."

"And that's the real reason you're renting that room. It's not because of the work placement."

He nodded, wiped his eyes. "Look, I'm really feeling down right now. Let's stop talking. It's only a few days before Christmas. Let's go to The Cave and have a good time, let loose. I don't want to think about him tonight."

"Okay," David said, squeezing his shoulder. "You're on."

"So, do you think it should go in that corner or over there?" Joyce asked him.

Sundar stretched out in the easy chair, a glass of coke in his hand. The Jets were playing the Panthers, and his team was getting creamed. "Put it wherever you like," he said, his attention on the screen.

Suddenly Joyce bounded over to him and landed on his knee. He looked up at her, tried to smile. "What?"

She smoothed back some of his hair. "I need help. The movers will come in January, and we don't even know where to put all my stuff."

"It's not a big house, Joyce. We may have to store some things. Oh damn, there they go," he skirted his head around her. "The Panthers are screwed."

She sighed, got off his lap. "I got to get ready for work. I was hoping we could…" she checked her watch. "Join me in the shower."

He would have really rather watched the end of the game but Joyce dropped all her clothes in a pile beside his chair and raced off giggling into the bathroom. He sighed and put his chair into an upright position.

"Baby!" she called out, turning on the shower. "Come on, I'm horny."

Sundar removed the rest of his clothes and slid back the shower door. He stepped in behind her praying for a hard on. It had been tough lately and he had no idea why. He wrapped his arms around her and began to touch her, knowing just where to put his hands to elicit the right response. He closed his eyes. *Xander.* He still dreamt about fucking him. It was bloody ridiculous but at least it did the trick.

"Um, baby, you're so hard," Joyce murmured.

"You don't like the show?" David asked, leaning forward across the table to talk in his ear. The music was loud. The whining guitar riffs which played over and over in his head were giving him a headache. Two men performed up on the stage. One was gagged and bound, the other tormenting him by running a feather up and down his dripping erection. Ordinarily it would have turned him on. Tonight? It was putting him to sleep.

"It's fine. I need some air." He stood, made his way through the standing crowd of excited men and found the exit. The night air was cool and still. Xander took out a cigarette and lit it with shaking hands. The smoking had been recent. If he could blame anyone, he'd blame Sundar, but he knew it had been his choice. He closed his eyes, inhaled the smoke, contemplating giving it up. He needed a drink. He needed to hail a cab and find Sundar. He just wanted to see him, talk to him. Yeah, they'd talk, have a cup of coffee. Who was he kidding? That's not all he wanted. He wanted to feel his naked skin against his, kiss his mouth, touch his cock, guide it up inside of him and hold it there forever. "God damn you, Sundar," he croaked. "What have you done to me?"

David came out now. He reached for the cigarette and took a drag off of it. "It's cold out here. Want to go?"

"Yeah. Let's find a room." He took his cigarette back. "Take me somewhere and fuck me."

His companion smiled. "Let's go."

"So ah, Joyce," Sundar said as she crawled into bed beside him.

"Um?" She cuddled up beside him, ran a hand over his chest. "What baby?"

"What do you want to do for Christmas? My mother wants us to come for dinner and…I didn't know what to tell her. If you want to go home to Texas, I'm okay with that."

"I'd love to introduce you to my family. Why don't we go to your parents at Christmas and fly out to Texas for New Year? My sister will flip when she sees you. She thinks she married the best looking man in the U.S."

"I don't have enough time off," he said. "I only have Christmas day. I'm working New Year's."

"Shit. How come?"

"You have more seniority than me." Joyce was five years older than he was.

"Damn. I can pull strings."

"No, I don't want to piss anyone off. You go to Texas. I'll come with you another time. Maybe you can meet my folks at New Year's.

"Um, okay," she said sleepily. "I'm so relaxed. Baby, you fuck like a champ."

He kissed the top of her head. A few minutes later she was asleep but he lay there with his eyes open staring at the ceiling. *Make this work, Sundar. She's good for you, smart. You can make her happy. It will be alright. It will be alright.*

Faggot. Are you...are you...are you...faggot? Want to fuck me, Sunny? Look at me...look at me.

"Sunny? Sunny?" Someone was shaking him.

He opened his eyes to see Joyce standing over him. She was holding a cup of coffee.

"You were dreaming. Are you alright?"

"Yeah, fine," he blinked, taking the coffee out of her hands and sitting up.

"What were you dreaming about?"

"High school."

She laughed and walked to the mirror. She began brushing her hair. "What were you like in high school?"

"I was a football player."

"Really?" she turned and looked at him, smiling. "Were you good?"

"Yeah."

"Who's Mark?"

"Mark?"

"Yeah, you said Mark in your sleep."

"He was a football player too."

"Oh. Were you friends?"

"No, not really."

"I'm going to make us some eggs," she announced and left the bedroom.

Sundar sipped the coffee. He remembered standing at the locker, dropping stuff so that he could lean down and spy on the boys soaping themselves in the showers, especially Mark, who he'd had a big crush on. His cock would get hard, and stay hard for a long time after. He knew it wasn't normal. He knew he wasn't like the other boys. But no one suspected, except Mark, who he realised now must have also been struggling with his sexuality. But nothing ever happened between them, nothing except for a lot of teasing and exhibitionism. He thought he'd buried all that deep inside, filed away under adolescent nonsense, until Xander.

He ran his hand over the sheet, remembering what they'd done here in this bed, how he'd fucked him, how Xander had moved under him, matching his pace. *Desire.*

"Eggs are ready!"

Sundar realised the coffee in his cup had grown cold. He'd just been sitting there staring into the cup all this time, long enough to allow Joyce to make them breakfast. He had to get a grip.

"That was fantastic last night," David said, standing in front of the mirror and trying to straighten his hair without the use of a hair brush. "You're so hot."

"Are you talking to me or your image in the mirror?" Xander teased, falling back onto the pillow.

"Very funny. Aren't you getting dressed?" He looked at him.

"Sure. Go get us some coffee somewhere okay and I'll be ready when you come back."

"Okay," he saluted and left the room.

The sex had been hot, rough, and he'd come, letting David dominate him in his usual way, first with a light spanking and then binding his hands. David was good at that and for awhile it had distracted him from the emptiness. When they settled down to sleep, Sundar was there with him again in his mind. He was standing at the kitchen counter, his sweatpants down around his ankles and Xander was sucking his cock. He looked up into those eyes and those eyes stayed with him until finally sleep was merciful and he faded off in oblivion. He could have sworn that the taste of him was still on his tongue.

With a groan he started to pick up his clothes. It was tough knowing Sundar was in the same city. He knew where he lived. He could probably look up his number in the phone book, get David to drive by his house, but he wouldn't. He wasn't going to become his stalker.

He took a shower, was met with hot coffee and doughnuts when he came out. He dressed and breakfasted at the same time. Finally, he said, "Let's go. I need to get back home."

"You do feel better, don't you?"

"Sure," Xander gave him a brief kiss. "Thanks, David."

"You'll forget him soon enough." He gave him a meaningful look.

Xander nodded. "Of course I will."

"You should call that woman and tell her you found another room."

"No."

"You're just asking for…"

"David, I've decided."

"Suit yourself. Listen, do you mind if we stop by one of the malls on the way out, I need to pick up a Christmas gift for my little brother, and I couldn't find what I wanted at home."

"Sure, no problem. Maybe I can find something for Nathan at the same time."

"Shopping?" Sundar groaned. "Is that why you're being so nice to me and feeding me?"

She cuffed him across the head. "No."

"Ouch. Okay, what do I need to shop for again?"

"My Christmas present for one thing."

He smiled. "Oh."

Joyce sat across from him and poured herself a second cup of coffee. "What are you getting your parents? Or rather, what are we getting your parents? I'll go half."

"I have no idea."

"What do they need?"

He yawned and sat back, pushing back his half eaten breakfast. "New windows."

She laughed. "Besides that! Does your mother wear perfume?"

"Yes, but my father buys her that. He'll be pissed if you do."

"Can't have that," she laughed. "Anyway, you need to look around, get some ideas. And whose name did you pick at the precinct for gift exchange?"

He made a face. "The captain's."

She started to laugh.

He threw his napkin at her. "So, what am I supposed to get the captain for fewer than twenty dollars?"

"A blow up doll?"

"Ha, ha."

"Get him some mittens." She stood up and took her plate to the sink. He followed suit.

"Mittens?" he wrinkled his nose.

She laughed again, turned and put her arms around his neck. "You're gorgeous, you know that?"

"I'm supposed to say that to you."

"But men can be beautiful, and honey, you're one beautiful boy."

"Boy now?" he made a face.

She kissed his mouth softly. "Um, all man, but sometimes you sound like a little boy. Go on," she said, slapping him on the butt and giving him a push, "get your coat and let's go shopping."

He groaned. "Yah hoo."

"Santa Claus looks like he tied one on last night," Xander commented as he and David stood in the middle of the mall watching the kids crawl up on Santa's knee.

David laughed. "Probably did. Candy cane liquor."

"Very funny. Let's go and find that toy for your brother."

"Have you decided what to get Nathan? What about the pharmacist?"

He shrugged. "Maybe I should buy them something together. I don't have much money this year. Any ideas?"

"A toaster?"

"Yeah, right," Xander muttered, following David as he headed off in the direction of the toy store."

"The rings are beautiful," Joyce commented as she paused in front of a jewellery store and gazed into the display window. "Look at the size of that diamond, Sunny."

Sundar felt his stomach tighten. "Yeah, it's nice," he managed, looking around. "Hadn't we better…"

Suddenly a clerk appeared at the door, a kindly looking woman of about fifty. She smiled at them. "Looking for an engagement ring?"

"No," Sundar said, shaking his head.

"Maybe," Joyce grinned, elbowing him, "if I could get him to propose."

Sundar cleared his throat.

"What a handsome young couple you make. Want to come in and try on some of the newest models?"

"Could we?" she looked at him.

"Joyce," he began but she was already in the store. He followed reluctantly. He'd never said anything about marriage.

Joyce pulled a stool up to the counter and the clerk opened the display. Sundar stood back, feeling quite helpless in the situation. He didn't want to embarrass her but damn it, this wasn't fair at all. He'd discuss it with her once they got out of the store.

Xander paused when he saw the sign up ahead for the Crown Jewellery Store. He knew that Barbara wanted a new jewellery box for Christmas. Maybe he could find one she liked in there that didn't cost a fortune. "David," he said, "you go on ahead to the toy store. I'll meet you there. I'm just going to look in the jewellery store for a few minutes."

"Okay," David said over his shoulder.

Xander was happy David had suggested a trip to one of the bigger malls in Raleigh. The place felt like Christmas with its bright decorations and Christmas carols. Even seeing Santa had been fun.

He continued on, feeling rather light-hearted as he walked into the store. He paused to examine several trinket boxes that were on display in front, picking up his head when he heard a woman squeal, "Oh Sunny, this one is exquisite."

There he was—Sundar—and he was staring right at him. Their eyes met and Xander didn't know what to do. Part of him wanted to run, the other part wanted to walk right up to him and...and what? Kiss him? Pound the shit out of him. The woman trying on rings had to be Joyce. Tall, brunette, beautiful, and looking at Sundar as if the entire world revolved around him.

Xander was frozen. It was Sundar who made the move. He excused himself to Joyce whose attention returned to the rock sitting on her finger and walked over to him. "What are you doing here?"

Xander could hardly breathe. Here he was, standing right in front of him, looking at him with those beautiful yet unreadable dark eyes. "Shopping."

Sundar nodded.

"Joyce?" He indicated with his head.

"Yes."

"Are you …are you getting married or something?"

"Married? No." He shook his head.

"Oh." He looked around. "Well, I got to go," he muttered.

"Xander," he began, "I…" but he was interrupted suddenly as the woman joined them.

Joyce linked her arm with Sundar's and smiled at Xander. "Hello."

"Hello," he managed. She was beautiful.

"Aren't you going to introduce me? Friend of yours?" she asked Sundar.

"Yes, I mean, we…" Sundar began.

"We met when he was on the job," Xander decided to try and rescue him. "He ah…"

"Gave him directions," Sundar interrupted.

"Yes, something like that." Xander looked at the floor. "Well, sorry, I have to go." His heart was pounding in his chest. He couldn't look at him. "Someone is waiting for me." He turned around and forced one foot in front of another then practically ran out of the store.

Joyce was staring at him a little too intensely now, and Sundar was in no mood to be interrogated. "Save it for felons," he grumbled. "Let's get out of here."

Joyce walked silently beside him until they reached the exit. "I didn't really get to do what I came here for."

No, he felt like telling her, you didn't because you spent all that time trying on bloody rings! "If you want to stay, I'll swing back and pick you up."

"Sundar?"

He looked at her.

"You've been acting weird since we met your friend back at the —"

"He's not my friend. Now, are we staying or going?"

"I'll come back on my own," she snapped and brushed by him.

Sundar sighed as he followed her out the door. At the car, he apologised.

She didn't acknowledge the apology.

"Okay, so it's the silent treatment." He got behind the wheel and started the engine.

"He looked really upset."

"Who looked upset?"

"That guy back in the …"

"I arrested him a while back, okay, that's probably why. Bad memories. Could we drop it? He's not important."

"I'm sorry for acting like that."

He glanced at her. "Joyce, I really didn't…I mean, I'm not ready for marriage. I'm barely ready for what's happening between us right now. Please, don't go too fast here."

She lowered her head. "I got carried away. The rings were beautiful and…"

"I know," he said softly, reaching over and touching her cheek. *Damn it, woman, why can't it just be sex and fun…why so fucking serious?*

"I love you, Sunny. I'm not sure you could say the same." She looked at him.

He drove out of the parking lot, keeping his eyes on the road.

"I think I fell in love with you the first time I saw you, on your first day on the job."

"Joyce." He didn't know what to say.

"It's all right if you don't feel the same right now. I can wait."

But she shouldn't have to. Why did he have to see Xander now? He was trying to put his life together. He didn't need this. He reached over and took her hand, smiled at her. "When you leaving for Texas?"

She looked at him hopefully. "I haven't booked yet."

"Maybe I can talk the captain into switching my time off."

"You mean it?" she grinned.

"Sure."

"What about your parents?"

"Well, they'll be a little upset but I'll spend some time with them at New Year's, even if it isn't right on the day."

"How are we going to handle the no fraternizing rule?"

"We're not going to say anything," he laughed, stopping at the light.

"So, why did you change your mind about coming with me to Texas?"

He shrugged. "I don't know." All he knew is that suddenly he wanted to get away from this town. The further, the better.

"So, are you going to tell me what's wrong?" David asked him on the way back to Cary. "You haven't said a word since we left the mall."

"I'm tired, that's all."

76

"I'm really happy we stopped. My brother is going to love—"

"He really thinks he can just make it all go away."

"Who?"

Xander glanced out the window. The big cedar in front of the city hall had been decorated with Christmas lights. It looked very nice, very festive. "I can't go and live there now."

"Xander!"

He looked at David who had pulled off to the kerb in front of the Freeda's Coffee Shop.

"What are you talking about?"

He opened the door of the car, paused, and then looked back at him. "Did you know that Sundar means lover?"

"Sundar again."

Xander got out of the car.

David followed on his heels. "I thought you were going to try and—"

"I ran into him and his girlfriend in the mall. They were checking fucking engagement rings." Xander threw up his hands.

"He's in the closet. He's going to stay there. Forget him."

"Easier said than done."

"He can't be that good in bed!" David said under his breath.

Xander closed his eyes for a second then reached for the door of the coffee shop. "I'm hungry."

"Good, I'll buy you a piece of cake."

Xander glanced at him. "Chocolate."

"You got it, babe," he said and gave him a brief hug before going up to the counter.

Xander watched him as he waited for the coffee. Okay, David was a bit eccentric but they enjoyed being together. Why couldn't he just fall in love with him?

Chapter Four

His mother stopped sniffing when he told her that he was going to Texas with Joyce. In fact, she beamed like a Cheshire cat. "So, it's serious?"

He shrugged.

His mother hugged him. "Then you're bringing her here for New Year's?"

"We both have to work New Year's," he told her. "I had to practically beg Roger for three days off at Christmas. He wasn't happy. But, the weekend after New Year's, we'll both be off so we can come for a meal then."

"Your mother's sister and stuck up husband are coming for Christmas anyway," his father said suddenly. He'd been sitting in front of the television watching the evening news. "She'll be plenty busy."

"Darren is not stuck up," Sophia protested. "You just don't like him because he used to work for Native Affairs."

"Native Affairs," he grumbled. "Imagine that."

"Ignore him," she said to Sundar. "Anyway, I am a little disappointed but it's for the best. You can get started on my grandchildren."

"Mom," he sighed, "slow down. No grandchildren. We're both busy. We have no time for kids."

"Yeah, don't encourage him, Soph," Clinton said. "He'll be having the brats over here all the time. You'll be stuck babysitting."

"He'd love it," she giggled.

"Well," Sundar lifted a hand to his father who waved him off, his gaze never straying from the TV, "I'm off."

"Don't get shot," he called out.

Sundar shook his head. "I'll try not to."

His mother walked him to the door. "I want you to be happy," she said.

Happy? What in hell was that?

He nodded at her and walked outside.

"Come by before you leave. We have your Christmas present."

"I will. I have yours too," he called back, as he pulled open his car door. It looked like it was going to snow. They usually didn't get much but still, it caused panic. He hoped it held off until his shift was done.

The phone rang several times before Xander heard the familiar voice of Sundar's mother. "Mrs. Kingfisher?"

"Sophie. Hello Xander. I recognised your voice. You wouldn't be free to move in at Christmas, would you?"

"Ah, no, I…actually, that's what I was calling you about." He really needed to put distance between Sundar and himself. He knew now that living at his parents' house would be a very bad idea.

"Xander, I am childless for Christmas. My sister and brother in law will be here, but with no young man in the house…I make a really good Christmas dinner and do you like—"

"Mrs. Kingfisher, I can't stay with you. I've found another place and…" He sighed, feeling really bad about the lie.

"No. I thought it was all settled. If you're worried about Sundar, he has nothing to say about this. I haven't told him or anything. Anyway, why should he mind? Is that why…?"

"Kind of. I don't want to cause a family feud or anything."

"Why don't you come for Christmas and we'll discuss it. Come see the room at least."

"I have Christmas dinner with my brother and his wife usually Christmas Eve and…"

"The dinner is on Christmas day here. I'll expect you at five. Is that all right?"

"Well, I…"

"Five o'clock. Once you see the room, you'll want it. I just know it. See you soon."

There was dead air in his ear. He sighed, closed his eyes. *Damn.*

An hour later he was sitting at the dining room table with his brother and sister-in-law, pushing the food around his plate. He jumped when Barbara asked him if there was something wrong with his food.

"Ah no, it's fine. I'm not very hungry, that's all."

"You've been moping," she added.

"I'm fine," he replied, his voice a little terse.

"Want to help me put up the Christmas lights outside tomorrow?" Nathan asked him.

"Sure," he agreed.

"Oh, Mike stopped by," Nathan added, putting a forkful of casserole into his mouth. "He said he'll call you later. I think he wants to go out for a beer or something. He's going skiing over the holidays."

"I don't know why you don't go with him," Barbara said. "You like to ski."

"Not really." He made a face.

"Mike would be much better for you than David," Barbara continued. "He's got a good job. He's handsome, very sweet."

"We're just friends, and David is just a friend too."

She nodded. "We just thought that there was someone."

"Well," he stood up, taking his plate with him, "there's no one. I'm going to call Mike."

"Xan," his brother said, "you can talk to us."

He nodded and headed to the kitchen. Shit. Was it that obvious?

He met Mike at what they'd nicknamed 'the old man's tavern' a little while later. Mike bought him a beer. They sat in a quiet corner, making small talk for at least twenty minutes before Mike said, "Is it David?"

"David?"

He and Mike had met once, but they'd never really hit it off. "He's not for you, Xan."

"I know that. We're just friends."

"But you're fucking him. Things get complicated when you fuck someone."

"I know."

"Then what is it? I've never seen you so down." He reached over and squeezed his hand.

Xander took a breath. "It's not David. It's Sundar."

"The closet guy?"

"Stop calling him that."

"Okay, the man you met who doesn't want to admit he's gay. Better?"

Xander laughed a little. "Not really. I think I'm in love with him."

"Nonsense. You were together what, an hour?"

"Two days actually, and we...well..."

"You made love."

"Oh yeah, we made love all right."

"And it was good."

"More than good."

"And then he kicked you out?"

"Not exactly, but kind of. He has a girlfriend, and I think he just decided to take her on. The other day I saw him and they were looking at rings."

"Ouch."

"Yeah, ouch."

"Let him go."

"I'm trying but his mother wants me to take a room at their house and..."

"Say no. That would be a mistake. Listen, he may deny what he needs all he wants but if you're nearby, sooner or later, he'll weaken and you'll end up in his bed again."

"Maybe that's what I want. Maybe that's why I accepted his mother's invitation."

"You want to be his whore?"

Xander closed his eyes. *Anytime.*

"Xander? Is that what you want?"

"I think I'd do anything to touch him again." He put up a hand. "Don't tell me the obvious, I know it all by heart, but I don't think it's enough to stop me. I want to be close to him, even if that means sleeping in his old bed alone. How nuts is that?"

Mike sighed. "Oh Xander, you got it bad, boy."

* * * *

Sundar stepped out of the car and wrapped his long dark coat around him. The lights of the ambulance were flashing on and off and several uniforms stood around the entrance to the bar. Charlie Pruitt, a seasoned uniform veteran had been the first one on the scene. He stood close to a young man in his thirties, who was leaning against the wall, his hands cuffed in front of him.

"What do we have here?" Sundar asked him as he glanced at the man in the cuffs and then over to the ambulance.

"Assault, provoked," he muttered. "The two others are inside the cruiser. They stuck their noses into it, of course. Real crusaders."

"Who's the victim?"

The officer took his elbow and pulled him aside. "Some degenerate little queen, name of Carl Sutherland. He apparently walked into the bar, and hit on Joe Riley here. Riley warned him to back off a few times, he refused and they got into it."

Sundar narrowed his eyes. The ambulance wasn't moving. "He's dead?"

"Was already dead when we got here. Owner called in a panic. That's where it gets a little messy. We got these two crusaders there in the squad car who decided they didn't want that kind in their bar, so they start beating on him, you know. Don't know really who did him in. Some of the witnesses say he could still stand until the other two took him outside into the alley."

Sundar walked over to the alley. He leant down to examine the blood. He sighed, stood and walked over to the ambulance. Two medics that Sundar knew were standing in front of the open doors. There was a body laying on a stretcher with a sheet over it. "Why aren't you taking the body to the morgue?"

"Officer Pruitt thought you'd like to have a look at the body before we took off, Sunny," Cindy Delmont told him.

Sundar hopped up in the back of the ambulance. "Cause of death?" He pulled the sheet down. "Fuck," he winced. "His face is a bloody mess."

"Yeah," she said, "broken ribs, smashed kneecaps, bruises. Guy was literally beaten to death."

Her partner Matt lowered his head. "Hell of a way to die."

Sundar stared at what was left of his face. He was young, too damn young to die just because he was trying to get laid. "Cover him up," he said, clearing his throat. He got out of the ambulance. "You can take him now."

"Okay, Sunny," Cindy's partner, Matt Selkirk said, "See you later."

Sundar stood there while the ambulance drove away.

Pruitt walked over to him now, his hat in his hand. "We're interviewing all the patrons, trying to get a clear idea of what went on. There were plenty of witnesses. What in hell was that fruity guy doing here anyway? This isn't no pansy bar. He was just asking for trouble if you ask me."

Sundar looked at him. "I didn't ask you."

Pruitt balked. "Okay, so sue me," he said, putting up his hand. "Getting mighty snooty since you took that exam, aren't you?"

"You're implying that he deserved it."

"I didn't say that. I just said —"

Sundar held up his hand. "Never mind that. Who are the two creeps in the squad car?"

The cop flipped open his book and rattled off some names Sundar thought he'd heard before. He'd have to check downtown.

"This might not be an isolated incident. This could be connected to that string of gay bashings we had a while back."

"I doubt it but then you're the hot shot detective."

"Let me take Riley with me," Sundar said. "We'll interview them all separately down at the station. I want the other two split up and taken in separate squad cars."

"You got it." He motioned to one of the other uniforms.

"Where's the manager?"

"Inside. He's shaken up."

"Put Riley in my car and put a uniform on him," he told Pruitt and then walked inside.

Rick's Place was a fairly respectable tavern where people went to drink away their troubles and play a friendly game of pool. In general, it wasn't much of a pick-up spot, gay or straight. He wondered what would have caused Carl Sutherland to go there. He was young, no more than nineteen, twenty, and there were gay bars in the city.

Rick Moth's hand shook badly as he lifted a glass of whisky to his lips. He was a mess, and he became even more of one when Sundar flashed his badge. "Detective now," he croaked, splashing whisky on the bar. "Wasn't bad enough with all those black and whites. This won't be good for business. People will think it's one of those fag bars."

Sundar clenched his jaw. "A man is dead, Mr. Moth, beaten to death. I think people getting the idea that this is a gay bar is the least of your worries right now."

"I didn't kill him. I tried to put a stop to it, told that fairy to leave. This is a respectable place."

Sometimes he felt as if he just shouldn't have gotten out of bed. "Okay, fine. Riley come in here often?"

"He's a regular. Good guy. Always pays, never causes no trouble."

"And the victim? Did you ever see him before in here?"

"Never. Like I say, isn't that kind of place here."

"Right. So, why would a guy like that come in here?"

He shrugged. "Damned if I know. He wasn't invited."

"And the other two who were involved with the beating…they dragged Mr. Sutherland outside?"

He nodded. "That's when I called the cops."

"Not before?"

"No reason. They seemed like friends before."

"What do you mean?"

"They all went into the back room together."

"To do what?"

"I don't know. I didn't go in there. They rented it, private like, wanted to play pool I guess."

"Pool?"

"Yeah."

Sundar sighed. "Right. Okay, then what?"

"They came out fighting. The fight was justified. The fag…the…fairy boy tried to force his whatever on Riley. He was all over him when they came out of there, tried kissing him and such. Riley kept pushing him away."

"No shit."

"Riley was having a hard time of it."

"How did that work?"

"What do you mean?"

"Riley is about six three, one hundred eighty. The victim was no more than five seven, slight build, probably about a hundred and thirty five, forty at the most."

"He went mad this guy, eyes a blazing...crazy like."

"Was he drunk?"

"No."

"Drugs? Did you see him use anything?"

"No, but...these people aren't right in the head."

"These people?"

"Fags...fairies...sissy boys. You know?"

Sundar inhaled some breath. *Keep your cool.* "Okay, you'll have to come down to the station. We'll need to have a statement from you."

"Do I have to close the bar?"

"Forensics will try and collect what they need as quickly as possible then you'll be able to reopen. We'll talk more downtown. And if I were you," he eyed the half drunk glass, "I'd lay off the booze."

He gave some more instructions to Pruitt and then climbed into his car. Riley sat cuffed in the back seat. He noticed as he was walking to his car that one of the others in the squad car opposite nodded at Riley through the window.

Sundar started the engine and glanced at Riley in his rear view mirror. "Hello Riley, we have some talking to do." He drove out of the parking lot and onto the road. "Where were you September 8th, around two in the morning? Were you anywhere near the Macdonald's Park?"

"I got nothing to say to you. I want to speak to my lawyer. And hey," he grumbled, "where in hell we going? This isn't the way to the police station."

"No," he said, "it's not."

It was cold putting the lights on even with all the sunshine they were getting. When they'd finished however, it looked great. "Come on," Nathan said, "get your skates. Let's go to the rink."

"Oh my God, I haven't skated in years," Xander protested but he was excited at the prospect of spending time with his brother.

They went to the inside rink and skated for an hour then Nathan took him for lunch and they did some last minute shopping. Tomorrow was Christmas Eve. On the way home in Nathan's truck, Xander mentioned going to Raleigh for Christmas dinner.

"Why?"

"I was invited by the lady where I'm going to be staying."

"Are you going to move in early?"

"I think so. I mean," he paused, smiled, "never mind."

"What?"

"I can't. Barb would kill me. You'll find out soon enough."

"Don't tell me she's pregnant again?" His face was white.

Xander laughed. "No. You'll see. You'll see." Barbara had confessed to him last night that she'd booked a trip to Jamaica over the holidays. It was supposed to be Nathan's Christmas present. Barbara's mother was going to come and stay at the house and look after the baby. He'd met Barbara's mother and he really didn't want to stay there with her. If he was going to take the plunge and move in with Sundar's folks, he might as well do it before he had another change of heart.

He was thinking of Sundar as his brother pulled the truck into the garage, feeling as if he should really fight for him, convince him, that if he didn't want him, that there was most likely another guy out there for him. What in hell was he saying? He'd kill any guy who tried to…

"What's so funny?" Nathan asked.

"I'm thinking about murder."

"Ah, you're definitely weird."

Xander punched him and they came into the house wrestling like two boys.

Barbara laughed when she saw them. "Okay, come have eggnog," she invited.

"Double rum in mine," Xander sang out.

"Me too," Nathan echoed.

* * * *

"So how long are you planning on keeping me out here in these woods?" Riley demanded. "This is sleep deprivation. Qualifies as torture, you know. I have a right to see my lawyer."

Sundar had called in to say that he had some car trouble and that he'd be in with the suspect as soon as the car was repaired. After that, he turned off his radio, knowing the captain's shift was over. It was almost supper time now. His stomach was growling and he was exhausted but he knew Riley was worse off than he was, plus he was pissing his pants.

"They will never believe that bullshit about your car breaking down? And I'll tell 'em…"

"You'll tell who, what?" Sundar turned around and looked him in the eye. "Because you haven't told me shit. And until you do, we'll sit out here in these woods."

"You're nuts."

"Yep." He turned back around.

"I've told everything. He came onto to me. I told him to back off. He didn't. We got into it. He walked out of that bar with those other two and after that…"

"You baited him. You lured him there."

There was silence.

Sundar turned around again. "You lured him there and you planned to punish him, show him what happens to gay boys when they run into real, big, macho men like you. Then when he came to meet you. You all took him into the back room, had a good time. I wouldn't be surprised if you raped him. Then you rejected him, humiliated him in front of the others. When he tried to leave, you hit him, and the other two, your buddies, finished him off in the alley."

"I don't know what…"

"While we've been sitting here enjoying nature, I remembered where I knew the names of the other two from. One of them was a member of the Klan, the other a loser who slithered away last time from a gay bashing in the Macdonald Park. Somehow they got you involved but you didn't know they'd kill him. You thought you'd have a little fun, that's all, because deep down, Riley, you're a bigger fag than Sutherland ever was."

"You fucking son of…" he tried to move forward but he could do nothing.

"Here's the deal. You admit what you did so I can get those other two pieces of shit and put their asses in jail where they'll really be in for a treat, and I'll make sure you do easy time."

Riley sat back in the seat, closed his eyes. "I really didn't think they'd kill him," he murmured.

"Well, life is filled with surprises," he mused, starting the engine. "Like this car for instance. It's a miracle but there doesn't seem to be anything wrong with it after all."

Joyce was very upset with him when he came into the station with Riley. "Where in hell have you been? The Captain is fit to be tied and God, I was so worried, Sunny."

"I'm fine. I'm going to lock him up now. He needs to sleep, eat. I'll get his statement before I go home."

Roger Colts stood at the door of his office, his massive arms crossed. "Sunny, what is this shit about having car trouble?"

Sundar walked into his office and grimaced as the door slammed behind him.

"When I was bringing Riley in, I had car trouble."

"For over fifteen hours? And why didn't you just call a patrol car? What in hell were you doing with a suspect for—"

"Tonight wasn't an isolated incident," he said, leaning forward. "Riley was a pawn in a game by the other two, who have been involved in a series of gay bashings in the area. I knew if I could be alone with Riley, I could break him."

"Did you?"

"Yes," he said, "but I offered him a deal."

"You can't do that. Only the D.A. can do that."

"I'm sure they'll go for it. Two serial bashers for one idiot bigot. It sounds like a good exchange to me."

"You got personal on this one, Sunny. This job will kill you if you do that."

He stood. "Point taken."

"Good work," he said.

Joyce was waiting for him when he walked out of Roger's office. "I don't have time for this, Joyce," he held up a hand, "I need to get a statement before—"

"You don't seem to give a shit that I thought you were in trouble or dead or...whatever!" She threw up her hands. "Jesus Christ, Sunny."

"I'm sorry."

"Are you going to tell me what's going on?"

"I will later." He walked over to his desk. "Promise."

"You look kind of sexy with that shadow though," she smirked.

"Guess I'm forgiven then." He grinned.

"Remember, I booked our flight. It leaves tomorrow morning at six."

He groaned. "Six?"

"What's wrong?"

"I haven't slept and by the looks of it, I'm not going to."

"You can sleep on the plane."

"Damn it, I haven't even brought over the Christmas presents to my parents. I thought we'd be leaving later. Why so early?"

"I wanted to make the most of the time you have. You'll have to leave the day after Christmas. And you can drop off the gifts tomorrow on your way to the airport. We'll have to bring both cars given that I'm staying through New Year's."

"You expect me to drop off my parent's gift at four in the morning?" Granted it was a pre-paid contract for new windows but he didn't feel good about leaving that in the mailbox. "Okay, I'll work it out," he said. "I got to get to the interrogation room," he muttered.

When Sundar finally got home, it was after midnight. There were no calls on his answering machine which meant his mother was giving him the silent treatment. She'd expected him to drop by earlier that day. The silent treatment was intended to make him feel guilty, and with that simmering guilt, he'd of course have to make retribution. "Damn it," he sighed as fell onto the bed and closed his eyes. He didn't bother undressing or getting under the covers. Exhaustion, that's what it was, but it was coupled with satisfaction, which was a great sleep inducer. Riley squealed on his two gay bashing friends, and now at least those animals were off the street for awhile. He didn't think about Texas, or Christmas, or even how guilty his mother was making him feel about Christmas. And he certainly didn't think about setting his alarm.

When he opened his eyes in the morning, he looked at the alarm clock that he hadn't bothered to set, and the first thing that dawned on him was that he'd missed his flight to Dallas. "Fuck!" He scrambled out of bed, not at all surprised to see that his answering machine was flashing, on both his home phone and cell. Personally, he was terrified to listen to the messages. He groaned. Joyce probably wanted to boil him in oil right now. He walked to the sink, drank some water and tried to think of what his next move should be. He could take a later flight of course, if Joyce was still talking to him. He looked at the clock. She was in the air. No point trying to call her and beg her forgiveness now. He'd try her cell phone about nine o'clock. He was tempted to go back to bed, but he thought he'd better check flight information and call his mother. At least he'd get to see them before he went to Dallas.

He took a deep breath and pressed the button on his home answering machine. "You have five messages."

"Five?" He moaned. He pressed the button and grimaced. Three were from Joyce. "Sunny, where are you? Do you want me to try and change the flight? Did you oversleep? Did you change your mind? Call me."

"Number one," he sighed. "Number two?"

"Sunny, fuck! They've just called for boarding. I've heard nothing from you? If you didn't want to go, you should have said. Damn it, Sunny…."

He pressed forward, that one was long. "Number three."

"Sunny, it's the captain. You need to get in here this morning. D.A. is up my ass."

Sundar ran a hand through his hair. That wasn't good. He listened to the last two, both from the captain. He picked up the phone. "Patch me through to Captain Green," he said when he got the operator. "It's Detective Kingfisher."

He was on hold almost five minutes before he heard Rogers' gruff hello.

"Hello Captain."

"Why aren't you in here?"

"I'm in Texas, remember?"

"You're calling from home."

"That's because I missed my flight."

"Are you and Detective Tucker doing the nasty?"

"Is that what you wanted me to come in for?"

"No. The D.A. says he can't make any deals for Riley. What did you promise that without—"

"Because the other two freaks are more important than Riley."

"He's got priors. He assaulted his wife two years ago, put her in the hospital."

"I didn't say he was an angel."

"D.A. wants to talk to you today."

"When?"

"Just get in here."

The line went dead. There were days, Sundar knew, that one just shouldn't get out of bed—and this was one of those days.

* * * *

The house was filled with people Christmas Eve, but Xander was feeling quite alone. He missed Sundar even though he told himself he shouldn't, and he was a little nervous about having dinner with Sundar's parents tomorrow. The expensive red wine Barbara had stocked up on had already helped a lot in soothing the ache.

Barbara was playing hostess to her well off friends and neighbours, while Nathan whispered to him, "She's in her element." He was doing his part in getting merry, swilling down Heineken with his buddies from work. Everything was perfect—the tree, the fancy trays filled with homemade goodies and the conversation. Barbara had even extended an invitation to David after some prodding by Nathan, and Mike, who'd always been welcome, brought his new boyfriend, a very flamboyant character who kept everyone laughing—and kept Barbara on edge. As it turned out, David was the least of her worries. He was quite quiet and sullen, probably due to Xander's confession that he was going to eat dinner at the Kingfishers the next day.

"So, what did you get for Christmas?" David asked him suddenly, coming over to where he stood gazing into the fireplace.

He looked nice this evening actually, dark pants and an open neck red shirt, not his usual garb. "Money," he said with a smile. "Nathan and Barbara gave me a money gift to help me get started in Raleigh. You?"

"A new watch," he showed him the oversized heavy metal watch he was wearing.

"Nice."

"My parents paid for my new tires as well. I'm looking for a better job."

"Still thinking about going back to school?"

"Maybe. Xander, we could have gotten an apartment together in the city. I don't think what you're doing makes a whole lot of sense. Does your brother know?"

"He knows where I'm going." Xander tried to sound irritated but he was.

"No, about this cop that you're fixated on."

"I'm not... Look, could we drop it. I don't want to talk about Sundar. In fact, he's the last person I want to talk about."

David gaze went to the staircase. "Want to go to your room?"

Xander smiled faintly. "Yeah." He grabbed a bottle of wine off the table and motioned to David with his finger. They ran up the stairs together.

Sundar was not in a good mood when he pulled into his parents' driveway. It was after ten o'clock and he'd been at the precinct until seven. He'd waited half the day to see the D.A., and more time was wasted playing tag with this person and that person. At the end, they had offered Riley a deal, but not one he seemed very happy about. Now, he was waiting to see his lawyer before he made a decision. If that shit head Riley didn't testify, those other two pieces of garbage he'd conspired with would probably do little time. Neither one of them had any priors.

If that wasn't bad enough, at around six o'clock, Carl Sutherland's father walked into the precinct. He demanded to know what was being done about the death of his son. He was irate, upset, and completely ignorant of whom his son was. "He's all yours," Roger told him on his way out. "I got a dinner party waiting for me."

It wasn't easy to tell an extremely emotional distraught father that his son was beaten to death because he was gay, and that the men who did it might walk out of jail with no more than a slap on the wrist. It didn't go well, and Sundar spent two hours sitting on a barstool in an empty bar listening to God damned Christmas tunes, and feeling sorry for himself.

Joyce wasn't answering her cell phone, and he still had the envelope with his parents' Christmas gift in the pocket of his coat. He was a little drunk when he walked up to the door. He chastised himself for driving like that, then knocked on the door. It took a few minutes. There was music playing, and his aunt and uncle's rental car was parked outside in the driveway.

The door opened and his father stood there. He laughed. "Whoa, is your mother pissed at you, boy."

"I missed my flight to Texas."

"Looks like you missed a few things. She thinks you left without…"

"I know. Well, you going to let me in or what?"

"How much you had to drink?"

"More than I should have. Merry Christmas."

His father opened the door. "Dorothy and the Tin man are here."

"Don't let Mom hear you say that," Sundar grinned.

"Ma," he called out, "Prodigal son is home, and he's sloshed."

"Thanks," he told his father. Sundar shrugged out of his long navy coat and walked into the living room. The Christmas tree lights were blinking on and off, and there was a fire roaring in the fireplace. His aunt and uncle sat on the sofa near the recliner where his mother was seated, and they were laughing about something.

His aunt was the first one to acknowledge him. She stood up and placed her hands on her mouth. "Oh my God, Sunny, you've changed. Look at you," she came over and placed a hand on his forearm, "so handsome and tall. You don't get your height from our side," she giggled. "Give your aunt a hug."

He leant down and hugged his mother's younger sister and shook hands with his uncle. His mother eyed him. He eyed her back with a bit of mischief in his eye, before making small talk with his relatives.

"So, come sit down," Dorothy said, "and tell us all about your job. Your mother tells us you're a hot shot detective now."

"Not so hot shot." He sat down in the other easy chair.

His father came in and handed him a drink. "Thought you could use this."

"Don't you think he's had enough?" his mother asked stiffly.

"Not when you get done with him, I don't."

Sundar laughed.

"Where's Joyce? Why aren't you in Texas?" his mother demanded.

"I missed my flight, police stuff got in the way."

"And she left without you?"

He shrugged.

"These independent women," his father muttered.

"Shut up, Clinton," Sophie snapped. "Are you going to Texas, or not?"

"Not," he said. "I've tried to call her and I get no answer...so..."

Sophie looked at her sister and brother-in-law. "Sundar is getting married but they're having a bit of a lover's tiff."

"We are not," he said, looking at his aunt and uncle. "Negative to both of those."

His mother ignored that.

Sundar drained his glass. Here he was, Christmas Eve, feeling twelve years old again, alone, with the entire world pissed off at him. He raised his glass. "Merry Christmas."

His father laughed and refreshed his drinks. "Looks like you're a shit out of luck tonight, son. And ah...give me your car keys."

"Why? You want to make an escape from Oz?"

Only his father laughed. Only his father understood what in hell he meant.

"You can't drive, Sundar," his mother said, getting up to refill the chip bowl.

"Had no intention of it."

"Good thing your room is still yours for tonight," his father announced.

Sophie looked at her brother-in-law. "Timothy, didn't you say that you wanted to travel to..."

"What do you mean, 'still' mine?" Sundar enquired. This scotch was going down really good.

"Nothing. You want your gift?" his mother asked.

"Sure. Mom, what did he mean..."

"I'll go and get it." She jumped up. "Dot, Tim, can I get you something?"

"No," they both said.

"That dinner was delicious, Sophie," Timothy commented.

"I must get your recipe for..." his aunt began, but his mother was already out of the room.

Sundar got up and followed her. "Hey," he said, watching her for a minute in the kitchen as she scooped more dip out of the container. "What are you doing with my room?"

"You're gone. You plan on coming home?" She glanced at him.

"No. But what did dad...?"

"Dad has a big yap."

"We've rented the room," his father said, walking into the kitchen. He popped some peanuts into his mouth.

"Rented the room? Why?"

"The house is empty," she said. "Anyway, it's my house and I'll do as I like."

"I didn't say you couldn't but you didn't rent my old room to a perfect stranger, did you? I mean, Mom, you have to be careful about..."

"Stop playing cop. He's perfectly nice. He'd going to be working at the hotel, part of his studies. Now, take the plate with the cookies out to the living room and pass them around."

Sundar sighed. "Have you thought this through? If it's money, I can help you out."

"It's not money," she snapped.

"We're good," his father said. "I'm going to have another drink. The Tin Man is going on about his family Christmases. I might as well puke due to the..."

"Clinton," Sophie threatened.

"I'm nice, I'm nice," he protested and left the room.

"Mom, I'm sorry about..."

"Me too," she smiled. "I just hope it all works out with Joyce."

"Why?" He narrowed his eyes. "Why do you hope it works out with Joyce?"

"I want to see you happy," she said, coming close to him. She touched his cheek. "You're not, you know. You're not happy. You have so much to give, Sundar. You're handsome, you're sweet, you have a good job. We raised you well. And I want you to have passion in your life, someone to come home to, who will love you and take care of you."

"Mom," he laughed, "I can take care of myself."

"I don't think so. Your heart, sweet boy, your heart. You haven't taken good care of that."

He swallowed.

"If Joyce loves you, she'll forgive you. Don't worry."

He nodded. He wasn't worried at all about Joyce, and that was what he was really worried about.

Xander was on his knees facing the wall and as David fucked him from behind, he slowly stroked himself. "Like that," Xander moaned, "okay, yeah, harder now...faster. Um..."

"Damn it, Xander," David complained, "maybe you should be fucking me."

Xander lowered his head. "Just-keep-going." He couldn't come. He saw Sundar's face in his head, but it was David's cock inside of him and he couldn't come.

David did. He came with a shout, bouncing back on the bed. "Oh yeah, that was...good."

Xander looked the locked door of his room. "Keep it down," he said. "Even with the party going on, someone could hear us."

David was lying back on the bed, his hand on his chest. "Who cares?"

Xander leant over and reached for his pants.

"You didn't come, did you?"

"Next time."

"It's the first time. And what was with all the specifics? Why did you have to be exactly in that position on that side of the bed and..." He stopped. "It's the way he fucked you, isn't it? You were trying to make me into him."

"No. And that would be impossible. You're not anything like Sundar."

David sat up. "I'm leaving."

"Why?"

"Because you used me. You didn't want me to fuck you. You wanted him."

"You got off, didn't you? It's never been more than that with us."

"Maybe I want it to be more." He sighed. "Forget him, Xander," he pleaded, reaching out to touch his cheeks. "We could be good together. I'm tired of playing around."

Xander got out of bed and did up his pants. "I can't, David, not when my heart is..."

"Obsessed with a man who is never going to be yours."

"You don't know that."

"Yes, I do. And so do you. Don't come crying to me when he uses you and throws you away." David started to dress.

"David, don't. Listen," Xander began, "I want us to be friends."

David did up his shirt. "I want us to be more. Merry Christmas. I'd say don't call me when it's over, but I'll probably be waiting."

Xander choked back the tears. "I'm sorry," he said, but David had already left the room.

Chapter Five

Sundar was half asleep when his mother walked into his old room and handed him the mobile phone. "It's Joyce," she said, with his eyes half open.

"Mom, I'm still asleep."

"She wants to talk to you. And your father went to pick up some clean clothes for you to wear for dinner." She pushed the phone into his hand.

His father poked his head in now, dangling a key. "I used the spare one, you know the one your mother keeps in case there is a sudden drought and you have no food in your house."

"Clinton," she chastised, pushing him out of the room, "Let's go. He needs to talk to Joyce in peace."

Clinton blew his wife a kiss and she swatted his rear on the way out the door.

Sundar shook his head and closed his eyes, sinking back down into the pillow. He had one hell of a hangover. "Joyce?"

"Sunny?"

"Yeah."

"I miss you. I'm not angry."

"You're not? I would be."

"You didn't miss the plane on purpose, did you?"

"I don't think so."

"What do you mean by that?"

"I didn't set the alarm. I was really tired. And as it turned out, I ended up at the precinct most of the day yesterday as well."

"How come?"

"D.A. crap. Anyway, no worries. And you? How is the family?"

"Good but disappointed. They wanted to meet you."

"They will."

"Did you spend Christmas there with your parents last night?"

"Yeah. I had a few, and I didn't even give them their present. Merry Christmas, by the way."

"You too. I wish I had you for Christmas. God, I was so horny last night thinking about your cock. Are you still there?"

"Yeah, I heard you."

"You think Roger will give you some more time off?"

"I'm not his favourite person right now."

"Oh. I have your Christmas present."

"You can give it to me when you come back."

"That's not all I want to give you, you big hunk."

He laughed. "Okay."

"I got to go. My sister still thinks she has the most handsome man, thanks to you."

"Sorry about that."

"Bye darling. I love you."

"Bye, Joyce. Take care." He hung up. Well, at least his mother would be happy. He rolled over with the phone and went back to sleep.

Nathan pulled his truck up in front of the two story ranch style house and nodded. "This is nice."

"Yeah. And Mrs. Kingfisher is a nice woman. I'm sure I'll like it here."

"Are you sure you don't want to wait for after the holidays to move in?"

"I want you and Barb to have some quality time together."

"You were never a burden, Xander," Nathan told him, meeting his gaze. "You're my little brother and I love you."

"I love you back, but you've done enough for me now. Time I make it on my own."

"And if you need me…"

"I'll call you," he grabbed his bag got out of the truck. "See you."

"See you," his brother called out. He blew the horn and drove on.

Xander stood staring at Sundar's Camaro, which was parked a little crookedly in front of the house. He must have left his car there for safekeeping while he was away. Parked nearby was another car, a blue sedan, a rental. Sophie told him that her sister and brother-in-law were coming for the holidays from Texas.

The house was lit up with Christmas lights and it looked very festive. For some reason, it did his heart good to be here. He felt close to Sundar and he liked it. As he walked towards the door, he noticed a garage on the left side of the house. The door was open and there was a man standing inside with his head under the hood of a nice looking jeep. When the man turned around, he knew it was Sundar's father. They didn't look a lot alike except for the black hair and dark eyes, but he had the stature, tall, muscular, broad shoulders, and he smiled exactly him.

"You must be Xander," he said.

Xander held out his hand. "Mr. Kingfisher."

He took his briefly. "Call me Clinton. Sophie's inside cooking up a storm. Just go on in. She's expecting you."

Xander heard the whinny of a horse. "You have horses?"

"Yes, four. Hope you like 'em. I used to breed 'em for racing and such. Now, they're mostly pets. Good riding animals. You ride?"

"No."

"We'll have to teach you then," he muttered, turned around and went back to the garage.

Xander knocked briefly on the door as he grabbed the handle and turned. Sophie was at the door when he opened it.

She smiled. "Xander, there you are. Come in." She gave him a hug.

"I'm not too early. It's only four o'clock, I—"

"Dinner will be at about six, if I can get my son out of bed. He's been sleeping all day."

"Your...ah son...I didn't know you had more than one."

"Just the one," she laughed. "Oh," she put a hand on his arm, "I hope it's not going to be a problem. I'm not sure I understand what the problem is between you and Sundar but..."

He never got the chance to answer. A voice suddenly blasted both of them into silence. "What are you doing here?"

Sundar stood frozen midway on the staircase.

"Sundar!" his mother snapped. "I didn't raise you to be rude. What is wrong with you? Xander is my guest."

"Guest?"

Xander looked at the floor.

"Yes, he's the young man I told you about. He's going to be staying with us."

Xander risked a glance at him. His stomach was in knots. Sundar couldn't have looked more shocked if he tried.

The grandfather clock in the hall chimed, shattering the terrible silence that had suddenly settled over them.

"Xander," Sophie said, "why don't you go upstairs to your room, first door on the right. Sundar, if you were nice you'd show him where."

Sundar walked down to the bottom of the staircase. "Well, I'm not nice," he replied with a strained smile and disappeared down the hallway.

"I'll...ah, find it okay on my own," Xander replied, his gaze following Sundar until he was out of sight. "I thought Sundar was in Texas."

"He missed the flight, but Joyce has forgiven him."

Xander nodded. *It figured that she would.* "I'll just stay in my room. I don't want to ruin your supper."

"Look, it's Christmas and Sundar will play nice. I'll talk to him. Don't worry. You just go on upstairs and take a look around."

Damn it. What had he done? He would have never come today if he knew Sundar was going to be here.

His mother was staring at him as he poured himself some coffee. "Where are Aunt Dot and Uncle Tim?"

"Playing pool in the basement, and don't you try and distract me." She shook her finger at him, never a good sign. "What is it with you and Xander?"

"Nothing. There is nothing with me and Xander. I hardly know the guy."

"Well, you had a pretty strong reaction to someone you hardly know. You don't like him. I want to know why."

"He's okay. We just don't...it's okay, Mother."

"You'll be nice to him at dinner then?"

"Do I have a choice? Why didn't you tell me that it was him who was renting my old room?"

"Because I didn't want to upset you."

"I would have known sooner or later."

"Um, check the turkey, will you?"

Sundar opened the over door. "Burnt to a crisp," he said.

"Is not." She slapped him on the arm. "Let me look."

He laughed. He had no choice but to laugh. He was so damn unlucky. The very guy he wanted to avoid most in the world would be sleeping in his old bed. How much irony could he take? *Put it in perspective. So, I fucked him once. He sucked my cock. It was nice. No, it was a whole lot more than nice. But it can't happen again.* But his cock was hard just thinking about it. He was going to get to hell out of here as soon as dinner was over.

The bed was unmade. Xander sat on the end of it and smoothed his hand over the duvet. He lowered his head to the blanket, inhaled. Oh God, yes, it smelt like Sundar. He'd slept here last night, probably a little drunk. He could smell that too.

When the door opened, he shot up into a sitting position, feeling foolish. Sundar filled the doorway with his tall, hard, well muscled body. He leant against the door jamb. Looking at him made Xander's mouth water. Flashes of being naked with this man seized him. He wanted him still. But from the look on Sundar's face, that wasn't going to happen.

"What in hell were you doing?"

"Nothing. What do you mean?"

"On the bed just now?"

"Nothing. I was tired. I was thinking about taking a nap."

"I'll change the sheets."

Xander shook his head. "No, it's okay." He wanted to sleep with that scent.

"What's going on? What are you doing here in my parents' house?" He met his gaze.

"I didn't plan this."

"Didn't you?"

"No," Xander snapped, standing. "I didn't. I'm not fucking stalking you if that's what you think."

"Keep your voice down. You're trying to tell me that it's just a coincidence that you're renting a room here."

"I met your mother that time when she brought over the lasagne. She mentioned she had a room, and I knew I was going to be needing one. I have a work placement at the hotel. It's for my diploma in hotel management."

Sundar didn't comment, so Xander pressed on. "I tried to back out later after we…well…you know, but she wouldn't hear of it." He sighed. "She misses her boy." He looked away. *So do I.* But Sundar was no boy, even if he was acting like one. "I understand that you're scared. You don't want people to know and…"

"I'm not scared, and there's nothing for anyone to know, nothing that's anyone's business."

"I won't tell anyone what happened."

"There's nothing to tell," he muttered. "Now, how long are you going to be here?"

"A few months." Something began to hurt deep down. Sundar was making it clear he wanted to be rid of him.

"Well, I'll try not to come around too much," he commented as he turned to leave the room.

"Sundar..." Xander heard his own voice fail. He reached out, almost touching his shoulder. "Please," he said softly. "I think I'm in..." He stopped.

Sundar glanced at him over his shoulder, waiting.

"Never mind. Listen if you don't want me to have dinner with you, I'll—"

"No, it's okay," he replied.

Xander suddenly found himself alone. "...love," he swallowed, finishing what he'd started to say a few moments before. "I think I'm in love," he repeated. He was trembling. He'd never been in love before, and he couldn't say he liked it much. It hurt like hell.

His mother went all out as she usually did for dinners like these. There was enough food for an army, with turkey and stuffing and cranberry sauce. Everything was perfect, except that Sundar had a hard time getting the food down. He'd done his best to put the night he and Xander had spent together behind him. And now, here he was, sitting across the table from him, making conversation with his aunt and uncle as if he was a member of the family. He was trying to put everything into perspective. Xander wasn't here to cause trouble for him. He was just renting a room from his parents. That's all. So why couldn't he just accept that and enjoy his dinner?

"So, how did you and Xander meet?" his aunt asked him suddenly.

"Meet?"

"Yes," she said, "Xander said you knew each other."

"I said we met briefly," Xander said suddenly, "and that Sundar was helping me with a police matter, and well,

Sophia came over at that time and brought food and..." He trailed off.

"He's a student," Sundar offered, staring down at his folk. "Mom likes having young men to pamper."

"I should be jealous," his father teased.

"Oh Clint," Sophia laughed. "Honestly. It's been empty since Sundar left, that's all. And Xander here is such a nice young man."

"You hardly know him," Sundar muttered.

"But I have good instincts. And any friend of yours is..."

"He's not my friend," Sundar announced, looking at her. He scraped his chair back and stood. "Excuse me everyone."

Xander was in shock. There was a lingering silence hanging around the table. He cleared his throat. "I apologise for Sundar. We've had a little misunderstanding recently. If you'll excuse me, I'll see if I can sort it out."

"I'm going to eat his dessert," his father said.

Xander glanced at Sophia on the way out of the dining room. She looked extremely upset. "God damn it, Sundar," he muttered, stopping at the bottom of the staircase. He could hear noise above. He was probably getting his stuff out of the room. As he climbed the stairs, he was relieved to hear things in the dining room gradually returning to normal. People were laughing and talking again.

Xander paused at the door to the room for a second then pushed it open.

Sundar glanced at him then returned to putting some of his stuff in a bag.

"What's all that stuff?"

"Stocking stuffers," he replied, concentrating on what he was doing.

Xander closed the door.

Sundar paused, looked up. "Leave it open."

"Why?"

"Because I asked you to."

"Because you don't want to be alone with me."

Sundar sighed, turned and looked at him. "Meaning?"

"Meaning you still feel something, and that's why you made a scene at the table."

"I didn't make a scene."

"Ah, excuse me. You made a scene." Xander met his gaze. "I still want you."

"Don't."

"Don't want you, or don't say it?"

"Both."

"Impossible." He moved closer. "I can't stop thinking about, Sundar. God knows I've tried. You put your brand on me that night. I'll never forget what you felt like inside me. I'll..."

Sundar raked a hand through his thick dark hair. "Stop."

"Fuck me," Xander pleaded, moving closer. "Take me somewhere now before I go crazy, and take me to bed for Christ's sake."

Sundar backed against the wall. Xander moved close enough to feel his breath. "You're so beautiful." He reached out and touched his cheek.

Sundar closed his eyes. "God," he moaned, his hand snaking down to his groin where he gently squeezed his own cock through the material. "I'm so damn hard."

"Baby, I can fix that," he gulped, pressing his body against Sundar's. He grabbed Sundar's wrists and lifted them up against the wall while capturing his mouth. They kissed deeply, moaning into each other's mouths as Sundar frantically ground his groin against his.

Xander found the strength to pull away, releasing Sundar's wrists. "Tell your parents, we're going for a ride to work out our differences," he breathed, looking into Sundar's eyes. "Take me back to your place."

Sundar's chest heaved. He went to say something but Xander quickly pressed his mouth against his. "Don't think," he murmured. "Act. I'll meet you outside. Hurry."

Sundar walked downstairs as if in a dream, hearing the front door shut as he did. "Mom," he said, walking into the dining room, "Xander and I need to talk about something. We're going for a ride."

"Where will you come back?"

"I...I don't know. Save me a piece of pie," he said and lifted a hand.

Xander stood beside his car, smiling when he saw him.

It wasn't going to matter, he thought, putting the key into the door and getting in as Xander got in the other side. After all, it didn't mean anything. It was just sex. Joyce didn't need to know. No one needed to know.

Xander placed a hand on his thigh as he drove. Sundar reached out and covered it, moving it to his cock. Xander took that as a sign of encouragement and undid the snap on his jeans and then slid down the zipper.

Sundar shifted a little in his seat, gripping the steering wheel. Xander pushed down his briefs and manoeuvered Sundar's cock out of his jeans.

"God, baby, you're so hard," Xander groaned as he let his fingers move over Sundar's shaft. "I just want to play with it a little. Can't I suck it while you're driving? Damn it, Sundar, I want it up my ass. I want to feel you inside me, Sundar, fucking me. Oh God."

Sundar glanced over to see Xander undo his own jeans. His hand slid down and began to stroke his cock while the other fondled his intensely. "How much further?" he breathed.

"Five minutes," Sundar managed his eyes on the road but his mind consumed with the sounds of Xander pleasuring his own cock. "Please," he pleaded. "Stop. I'll never make it."

"Okay," Xander grunted. "I'll be good." He bent his head and kissed Sundar's cock gently, and Sundar almost went off the road.

"Xander, fuck!"

"Okay, sorry," Xander appeased. "Just drive."

Xander was out of the car even before it came to a standstill. He watched Sundar as he got out and came towards the front door of the building. They walked upstairs. Xander kept his eyes on Sundar's firm round ass they climbed, his cock hard, his mouth dry. When the door was open and they were inside, Xander suddenly couldn't move. It was weird. What he wanted most was right in front of him, waiting, and he couldn't bring himself to take it.

"What's wrong?" Sundar asked.

"No…nothing. I…"

Sundar began to undo his own shirt. He threw it aside. Then he kicked off his boots and slid his jeans down over his hips. The underwear came down with them and he stepped out of them. He looked up at him suddenly, pushing his hair back out of his eyes. He smiled.

Xander swallowed. That smile went right through him. *You're going to be the death of me.*

"Coming?" He turned and walked off into the bedroom.

Xander nodded to no one but himself. He took off his boots and his coat and walked down the hallway in the same direction. When he got to the room, Sundar was stretched out on the bed, pillow under his head. His erection was standing up in the air in invitation and there was a look in his eyes that spoke of need and desire. It was intoxicating.

"Take off your clothes."

Xander held back a sob. He nodded and hastily undid his shirt and threw it aside. Next he pushed down his pants, grazing his swollen cock, which caused his entire body to shudder.

"You want my cock, come and get it. It's yours tonight."

Tonight. Only tonight? He came over to the bed and sat down. He let his hand wander over his chest down to his stomach. His fingers curled possessively around his shaft. "Mine?" He began to stroke it, bent his head to it and licked around the head. "Mine. Your cock is mine tonight—to do with as I please?" He glanced up at him, met his eyes.

Sundar licked his lips. "That's what I said," he grunted.

"And your lips?" He stretched up and kissed his mouth.

"Those too."

"These?" he insisted, twirling his finger around one of his stiff nipples then pinching it gently.

"Um, yeah."

"And your ass? Is it mine too?"

"You want to fuck me?" Sundar met his gaze intensely.

"Will it make you mine?"

Sundar narrowed his eyes.

"Tonight?" he qualified his voice barely above a whisper as he crawled up onto the bed beside him.

"Yeah, tonight."

Xander kept his hand on Sundar's cock. He kissed his mouth again tenderly, moved his hand through his hair as the other stroked and squeezed his cock.

Sundar moved his body, thrusting his hips up in the air.

Xander kissed down his chest, licking his nipples, and moved down to his belly. He knelt between his thighs now and pressed his mouth to Sundar's succulent cock, already leaking cum. He glanced at him, savouring the expression on his handsome face. "Tonight, you need me."

"Yes," he hissed. "I need you."

Xander swirled his tongue around the head of his cock then lowered his mouth down over it. He opened his jaw and took more of it into his mouth, sucking and licking while one hand snaked down under Sundar and slid between his ass cheeks.

Sundar's fist pounded the mattress as Xander intensified his efforts to bring him to orgasm. Xander could feel his cock responding to his every effort, tasted Sundar's juices in his mouth.

"Oh God, Xander, Xander, I'm …"

Sundar's cock pulsed in this mouth. Xander moved off of it, sitting back for a second, just watching Sundar's face contort and his body shudder with orgasm. "You're the most beautiful..." he began with a whisper, his heart feeling heavy suddenly, and sadness. *You're not mine. No matter what you say. You're not mine. You won't allow yourself to be mine.*

Xander moved up into his arms when Sundar quieted. Sundar drew him close, wrapped his arms around him and for a few minutes he seemed content just to lay there in his arms.

"What are you thinking about?" Xander asked him, tracing the line of his square with his finger.

"Nothing really."

"I don't believe you."

"Okay then," Sundar said, moving his hand down over his chest to his spent cock. "I'm thinking that I want to be hard again so that I can fuck your sweet ass."

"Oh." Xander smiled. "That I believe. I can help you with that."

"Um, I know," he replied.

Xander laughed softly. "Is that a compliment?"

"Could be."

Xander looked into his eyes. "Have I told you that you're a beautiful man?"

"I believe you mentioned it."

Xander hand slipped down to Sundar's cock. He brushed his hand away and began to fondle it himself. "How's that?"

"You have the magic touch."

"Do you have lube?"

"In the medicine cabinet. I'll go."

"No, I'll go," Xander said, crawling out of bed. "You're hard again."

Sundar looked down at himself. "Already?"

Xander laughed as he walked into the bathroom. "You're a stud."

"Yeah, right."

Xander laughed, switching on the light as he opened the medicine cabinet. The first thing he saw was a home pregnancy test and a package of tampons. His heart sunk. He took out the box with the pregnancy test and stared at it. "Is Joyce pregnant?" he called out suddenly. He'd blurted it out without thinking.

Sundar was suddenly standing at the bathroom door, beautifully naked and hard. "What?"

"There's a home pregnancy test here and…"

"Give me that," he muttered, yanking it out of his hand. "What the hell?"

"Looks like she wants to have your baby."

"Nonsense. We haven't even discussed that."

"Are you going to marry her?" Xander glanced down at the floor.

"I...I don't know." He put the pregnancy kit down on the counter.

"You were looking at rings."

"Joyce was looking at rings. Now, can we forget all that? Look what you've done to me."

Xander ran his gaze over the length of him.

"Want me?"

Xander nodded. "Oh yeah. There's no doubt about that."

"How do you want me?" he grinned, holding out his hand.

Xander laughed leaving the bathroom behind. "Take me from behind, on my knees like the last time." He was breathless.

"Your wish is my command, baby."

Sundar pulled Xander up onto his knees and back into his arms. He kissed his throat and his shoulder and used his one hand to stroke his cock. The other pinched and tugged at his nipples until Xander was butting his ass into his groin like a bucking bronco. With one finger, he took his time lubing Xander's ass, coaxing some deep moaning and pleading out of him before he decided that he couldn't wait anymore to be inside of him. He positioned his cock and pressed into his body, his arms wound tightly around his slender waist. Then he began to pump and they descended into a slow, sensuous pace that took him out of this world and elevated him to the place of angels. At least that's what it felt like. "Oh God, Xander," he whispered. "You feel like heaven." He pumped harder, Xander crying out something unintelligible as they both came, panting, and moaning.

"Sundar, I love you. I love you…baby….I love you."

Sundar bit his lip. He released him, pulled away. Those words rocked him right back into reality. *What have I done?* "You can't. You don't love me, Xander, shit. This is sex, that's all."

Xander was laying on his stomach now, his face on the pillow. He didn't reply.

"Damn it. Shit, why'd you have to ruin this?" He got up off the bed.

"Ruin it? Is that what I did?" He lifted his head.

"I don't want to do this."

"You don't want to do what?" Xander sat up. "Admit who you are?"

"I'm not gay."

"Not wanting to be gay doesn't make it so."

"Fuck you."

"Here we go."

Sundar left the bedroom.

Xander crawled off the bed with a heavy sigh. Words could lie but Sundar's body couldn't. The way he held him, the way he kissed him. "I know." Xander walked out in the kitchen where Sundar was getting a drink of water. "I know what I felt just now."

"Yeah," he said, drinking some water, some of it dribbling down his chin and onto his naked chest, "but you don't know what I feel."

Xander came over and took the water bottle from him. He traced the droplets that had fallen on his chin and his chest with his finger. "You won't let yourself feel. You'd rather spend your life with Joyce, who can't give you what

I can give you, so that you're acceptable somehow. But to whom, Sundar? Who in the hell are you trying to impress? Do you think your friends, your family will turn on you, won't love you anymore if they find out you prefer cock?"

He took his water bottle back. "Are you finished? This was supposed to be sex, a good time, and you had to turn it into..."

"I can't pretend like you."

"I'm not fucking pretending. I wanted you tonight. I had you. It's that simple. You don't need to read anything into it."

"You said you were mine tonight."

"Yeah."

"Well," he held out his hand, "the night's not over."

Sundar put down the bottle. "Fair enough. But no more love talk."

"All right." He swallowed his pain, allowed the sight of Sundar to gloss it over, blot it out. "I want to fuck you. Will you let me?"

He shrugged. "Sure."

"You're not afraid?"

"Why should I be?"

"Because it's your first time," he said softly.

"You don't know that."

"Yeah, I do." He took his hand. "Come on, I'll go easy."

Sundar took his hand. "I can take it."

"I know, macho man," Xander laughed.

It hurt like hell but he didn't cry out. He wasn't even sure why he'd agreed to let Xander do this, but somehow he knew that if he didn't try it tonight, he was never going to. And after the pain subsided, it actually felt pretty good, a strange mix of pain and pleasure. But it was the look on Xander's face after he'd filled his ass with his smooth creamy cum which seemed to really tip the scales in the favour of pleasure. It was like sunshine.

Xander clung to him, his body trembling, saying, "Thank you, thank you, thank you," over and over again.

Sundar kissed the top of his head and pulled him close.

"How was it?"

"It was okay."

"You don't like it much."

"I supposed it's an acquired taste. You enjoyed fucking me, didn't you? You like it more than being fucked?"

"No. I prefer to be the bottom but letting me have you like that was an incredible gift. Why did you give it to me?"

"I don't know. Maybe because I knew you wouldn't hurt me. Maybe because...look." He turned on his side and stared into Xander's face. "Joyce is coming back soon. I want you to understand that I'm trying to make a life with here. We can't do this anymore."

"What are you going to do with these feelings, Sundar?"

Sundar didn't offer an answer. He didn't have one.

* * * *

When Xander opened his eyes, he was alone. He looked at the clock and groaned. It was after ten o'clock in the morning. He checked for a note, nothing, but the answering machine was flashing. Maybe he'd called him and left a message. He was probably at work. He pressed the machine and waited. *You have one message.* The voice was female. "Hey baby, it's Joyce. I really miss you. I'm coming home earlier. I want to spend New Year's there with you. The family understands how crazy I am about you. I love you, Sunny. I miss you. I can't wait to rip off your clothes and ride that…"

Xander switched it off. He walked into the bedroom, and got dressed. Twenty minutes later, he left the apartment and went back to the Kingfisher's. Sophia asked him if he and Sundar had worked out their differences and he said yes and left it at that.

David knew something was wrong the minute Xander called him. "You didn't?"

"I didn't what?"

"You know what. You didn't fuck that cop!"

"Can we not talk about Sundar please? Want to meet me in the city, see a movie?"

"Sure. Which one?"

"Anything except romance."

"I hear you. I'll pick you up in a couple of hours."

"I'll give you the address," he said. He lay down on Sundar's old bed, hugged the pillow and fell asleep.

David arrived around eight o'clock and Xander was ready. He said goodbye to Sophia and Clint and walked outside with David, just in time to see Sundar's car pull into the parking lot. "Wow, nice car," David said, "who's that?"

"Just keep walking," Xander said.

"Is that him?" David asked as Sundar got out of the car.

"Yeah."

"Holy shit, no wonder you…"

"Shut up, okay."

They came face to face. No choice.

"Hey," Sundar said, looking at David. He nodded.

He had no choice but to introduce him, and suddenly, he wanted to throw David in his face, even if he knew it was childish. "Sundar, this is David. We're going to a movie. Any suggestions?"

Sundar's face was a mask of unreadable emotion. He lifted his head up. "I don't know what's playing. Have a good time." He walked past.

Xander swallowed. "You might have left a fucking note," he called out without turning around. "Come on, David, let's go. We don't want to be late for the movie."

In David's car, he cast a look towards the house. "He didn't even pause, didn't turn around, and didn't even say a God damned word. Do you know what he told me last night?"

"No," David sighed, starting the engine, "but I have a feeling you're going to tell me."

"He said he wanted to make a life with Joyce."

"But that's not a surprise. They were picking out rings that time in the mall."

"I found a pregnancy kit in the medicine cabinet. She wants to have his baby."

"Xander, stop this. Stop tormenting yourself. He wants to live his life a lie — there's nothing you can do. He'll find cock anyway, he'll just do what all the closet queens do. He'll hire male prostitutes and if he doesn't bring his wife back any disease, she'll never find out about it."

Tears rolled down Xander's face. "But he loves me."

"If he loved you, he'd be with you. He doesn't love you enough. Now, forget him."

"I can't."

"Well, stop fucking him. That would help."

"I can't do that either. I know that anytime he wants me, I'll…"

"Xander. Once the woman gets home, that's it. He'll play the straight eight boy, and you'll be left with your cock in your hand."

He wiped his eyes, nodded. "You're right. Do you think he was jealous seeing me with you?"

"Xander!" he cried out.

"I just wondered. He holds his feelings in and…"

"He's a cop. They're like that, cold, unfeeling pricks. Now, let's pick a God damned movie and enjoy ourselves, shall we?"

Chapter Six

The report took longer than he thought. Joyce was
already home and had left him several messages. And he
was still at the crime scene. A woman had been brutally
beaten and raped and left for dead outside an abandoned
warehouse. Forensics was still combing the scene and
Sundar was perplexed over a piece of evidence found at
the scene. He hadn't had any time to call her back.

At one in the morning he sat at a small out of the way
tavern and drank. His head was swimming with clues
from the scene, and in that sea of details was Xander with
that punk he was with tonight. What in hell did he see in
him anyway? He was a scrawny, skinny little runt with
makeup on his face. Christ, Xander could do better than
that.

He called for another drink and then figured that would
be it, one more and he wouldn't be able to drive. Hell, he
wouldn't be able to move. He checked his phone and saw
two new messages from Joyce. *Fuck!* He'd forgotten all

about Joyce. She'd be pissed at him again. He picked up his glass and laughed. Let her.

When someone nudged him at the bar, he was almost asleep. He expected it to be the bartender, harassing him to go home. He looked up to see a good looking blond man standing there, around his age. "Sunny? Sunny Kingfisher?"

He blinked, stared at his drained glass. "Yeah?"

"My God, I haven't seen you since high school. Do you remember me? I'm Mark, Mark Carr. We used to play football together."

Sundar glared at him. "Oh, just fucking great. That's all I need. I should smack you in the mouth," Sundar muttered, shaking his head then he began to laugh.

Mark took a step back.

"Don't worry," he waved at him and stumbled off the barstool. "It was a long time ago. I'm over it. Plus, I don't have the energy. So, you still jacking off in front of straight football players?"

"Let me give you a ride, Sunny. You don't look like –"

"Why, so you can jerk off in front of me again?"

"We were boys."

Sundar looked at him. "Yeah, boys." He pushed past him.

"Sunny, I can't let you drive like that. You're loaded."

"I'm not loaded, and you're not my keeper."

"We were friends," he said.

"No, we weren't friends." Sundar paused and looked at him.

"I've come to terms with who I am."

"Good for you. Who in the fuck is that?"

Mark put a hand on his arm. "What about you, Sunny?"

"It's Sundar. Why can't people say my fucking name? And I know who I am. Thanks." He pushed out of the exit door and stood in the parking lot looking for his car.

"Sundar?"

"You're still here?" he eyed him. "Get lost."

"Let me call a cab at least."

"Why did you do it?"

"Why did I do what?"

"Torment me like that?"

"I was tormenting myself. Hell, Sunny, you were so hot in high school, and now, holy shit…you've turned out to be one hell of a good looking man."

"Get on with it. I asked you a question."

"I was struggling. I wanted you. I just didn't know how to do it without coming out, admitting I was gay. It took me a long time to come to terms with it, Sunny."

"It's Sundar."

"Sundar. So, did you go through the marriage thing?"

"No."

"But you're out, right?"

"Mark, just fuck off. You're not getting laid tonight so forget it."

"That is a shame but that's not what I'm getting at. Christ, you're still in the closet," he accused.

Sundar swung at him before he'd even realised what he was doing. It finally dawned on him when he found himself looking down at the man lying on the pavement that he'd knocked the guy out. "Oh fuck," he groaned and went to his knees beside him to see what the damage was. Mark was breathing but out cold. "Fuck, fuck," he muttered, searching his pocket for his cell phone. Just as a voice came on the line, a siren could be heard in the distance. He looked up to see the bar owner standing in the doorway. Damn. He'd called the cops. Sundar put his head in his hands. The sobering thought of losing his badge came to mind. *What in fuck did I just do?* "Mark," he said, slapping the man's face gently a few times. "Please don't do this to me." There was blood coming from somewhere. Sundar put his hand under his head and it came away sticky. He could see a blood stain on the pavement. "Please, don't do this to me, you bastard. Don't do this to me."

He was shaking when the two uniforms walked over and one of them said, "Stand up slowly with your hands where I can see them."

Sundar glanced up at him. "I'm a cop," he confessed. "Detective Kingfisher, Sundar Kingfisher."

The officer looked shocked. "I know you. I'm Dan Montel. What in hell happened here, Sunny?"

"I saw everything," the bar owner called out, hurrying across the parking lot to join them. "This guy here," he pointed at Sundar, "he just attacked the other guy for no reason, went crazy."

Sundar managed to get to his feet, his hands out at his sides. He closed his eyes.

"Are you armed?" the officer asked him.

"No, search me if you like."

"Sorry about this, but..." he began to pat him down.

The other cop was kneeling beside Mark. "He's coming to," he said, glancing up as the flashing lights of the approaching ambulance illuminated everything.

Sundar closed his eyes when he heard that Mark was coming to. *Thank you, God.*

Officer Montel took out his notebook. "What happened?"

"He assaulted him, I tell you," the bar owner piped in.

"Jerry, take the man inside," Montel told his partner, "and get his statement.

The medics came over to where Mark lay and began to poke and prod him. He was conscious and mumbling something. The cop with Sundar took his arm and steered him off a few feet. "How do you know that guy?"

"We went to high school together."

"How much have you had to drink tonight?"

"Much."

"Obviously you had a score to settle. You popped him a good one."

"I didn't mean to hit him so hard."

"You're pretty drunk. You were intending on driving like that?"

"Look, don't play cop with me, Montel. I know the law. Just do what you need to do."

"You know what will happen if he presses charges."

Sundar sighed.

"If I were you, I'd talk to him before they take him to the hospital, see if he'll consider not pressing charges. Otherwise, you're in a heap of shit. If you can convince him, I'll pretend we never got this call."

"Why are you doing this?"

"Because you're one of us. And it looks like you're going through a bad time. Wife leave you or something?"

"No."

"I know someone who's fucked up when I see them. Better get it together. Now, he's awake. I'll give you five minutes to work it out."

Sundar nodded. "Thanks." He walked over to where Mark was sitting on the stretcher. He looked at the two medics. "Can you give us a minute?"

"Sure," one of them said, "but then we need to move."

Sundar nodded as they walked away.

Mark glared at him. "What in fuck could you possibly have to say to me?"

"I'm a cop. If you press charges, I could lose my job."

"You hit me, God damn it, because you didn't want to hear the truth."

"I lost my temper. I didn't mean to. And don't piss me off again."

"I could have helped you. I know what you're going through, Sunny."

Sundar reached out and grasped his hand. "Please," he urged softly. "Don't press charges. I'll do anything you want. I can't lose my job."

Mark placed his other hand over his. "Okay, but let me help you. That's all I ask. You were my high school crush, for Christ's sake. It's the least I can do."

He shook his head, pulled away. "I'll be all right. I'll pay for any lost wages or..."

"Medics say I'm going to be fine, may need a few stitches that's all. I'm sorry I tormented you in high school. I should have made a man out of myself and just told you that I wanted you. If it was now, I..."

"Don't mention it," he said gruffly moving out of the way as the two medics came back.

"Sorry, we gotta' move," one of them said.

Sundar nodded. "Go ahead."

Mark dug in his pocket as they began to roll the stretcher forward. He held out a card. "Call me. If you don't want me to press charges, I won't, but on the condition that you'll at least let me talk to you."

Sundar took the card, nodded, and shoved it into his pocket.

Montel and his partner drove him home in the patrol car. "You were lucky," Montel told him as they pulled up in front of his apartment building.

"Thank you," Sundar said as he got out. "I owe you one."

"I won't do it again. Whatever is eating at you, root it out before it really fucks you over."

"Where in hell have you been?" Joyce demanded as Sundar opened the door for her seven hours later. He was half asleep, his eyes burning, and he had one hell of a hangover. He didn't need this shit.

She pushed her way in the door and closed it. "You look like hell. Where were you last night? I must have called you a dozen times."

Sundar wrapped the blanket around him and went into the living room. He threw himself down on the sofa and closed his eyes.

"Sundar?" He could feel her standing beside the sofa. Her leg was brushing his. "Why aren't you talking to me?"

He forced his eyes open. "Because I've got a God damned hangover, if you must know, and I'd like to sleep. I don't appreciate the third degree, okay?"

"You've got to be at work in two hours. You're on days this week."

"I'm calling in sick." He sat up, crossed his arms.

"Are you sick? Who were you drinking with?"

"Myself. And yes, I feel sick, okay?"

"I wouldn't make waves with the captain if I were you," she sniffed.

"Well, you're not me."

"Is something wrong?"

"Yeah," he grunted, standing. "I'm tired and I want to sleep. So, leave me alone, okay?" He walked back into the bedroom and slammed the door. When he crawled onto the bed, he sunk the pillow over his head and closed his eyes. Xander's face smiled back at him and he groaned. "Go away," he muttered and tumbled back into a restless sleep.

Sophia seemed so delighted that he enjoyed his breakfast. She beamed like a schoolgirl. "Best breakfast I ever had," Xander told her, rubbing his stomach.

"Sundar always loved his breakfast."

Xander bit his lip. He would have loved to have had the chance to make Sundar breakfast; bring it to him in bed. *Sundar. I love you. Why do you have to be so stubborn?* "You'll have to let me cook for you sometime. I'm not bad."

"That would be fun," she said, pouring them both more coffee and then sitting across from him. "What's your breakfast specialty?"

"Waffles."

"Love those. With fruit?"

"Yeah, blueberry is good."

"Sound scrumptious. When Sundar was a small boy, he used to like me to make people pancakes."

"What are people pancakes?" Xander asked, laughing.

"Pancakes, shaped like people. You can draw faces and such."

"What was he like as a boy, Sundar?"

"A quiet, brooding little boy, very smart and athletic. Could have been all-pro in football if he'd wanted to but he got injured."

"He told me he screwed up his knee."

"Well, a player on the other team did it for him, to stop him from making a touchdown. There was a scout who had his eye on Sundar, but…well…never happened."

"Think he was disappointed?"

"I think he was for awhile but then he went to the academy and he fell in love and when Sundar falls in love with something, it's for good."

Xander bit his lip. "Like with Joyce?"

"I guess so, yet he hasn't brought her by here once. If she's going to be a part of this family, I'd like to meet her."

"So ah...Sundar is going to marry her?" He held his breath.

"I assume. I haven't heard any announcements yet but...I'm hoping for a grandchild. One would do."

He was just about to say something when the phone rang. Sophia got up and answered it. "No," she said, "he's not here, Captain. If I hear from him, I'll tell him you called. Is there a problem? Oh. That doesn't sound like Sundar. Did you talk to Joyce? Well, because she's his fiancée. Did you call his cell phone? No one answering there either? Usually he's pretty good as answering his cell phone. Okay, good-day Captain." She hung up and looked at Xander. "Sundar didn't go in to work today, and he didn't call in either."

"I hope he's all right."

"Not like him."

Xander got up. "I'll go and check on him if you like. Maybe his phone isn't working."

Sophia reached for her purse which was hanging on the door and opened it. She handed him her car keys. "Take the car. Call me when you get there. I'd go myself but Clint's out and the vet is coming to check on one of the horses."

"It's okay," he said, taking the keys. "I'll come right back."

"One of those keys is for his apartment," she said.

"I won't go in unless I suspect he's in trouble, Sophia. But I'm sure he's just fine."

Xander drove Sophia's small sports car well over the speed limit. He was worried. What if something had happened? He pulled to a stop outside Sundar's building and noticed that his car wasn't in the parking lot. He was out. He climbed the stairs and put the key in the lock. He'd leave him a note telling him to call his mother as soon as he got in.

He walked in and closed the door. He spotted a pen and pad near the phone and picked it up. As he did, his gaze drifted towards the bedroom where he and Sundar had made love. He longed to go in and just lie down on the bed, lose himself in the memory. Two minutes, that's all.

He put down the pad and paper and made his way to the bedroom. When he opened the door, he realised that the bed wasn't empty. "Sundar?"

He came closer and leant down to touch his shoulder. "Sundar?"

Sundar reared up on the bed like Dracula might in his coffin. His eyes blinked open and he looked confused for a minute. "Xander? What in hell are you doing here? How did you get in?"

He dangled the key in front of him. "Your mother sent me. Do you realise that your boss is livid? You missed work and didn't even call in."

He yawned, pushed his hair back. It didn't take much imagination to realise that Sundar was completely naked under those blankets. "What, you're walking into my apartment now whenever to hell you feel like it?"

"I told you, I have the key, and we were worried."

Sundar pulled the blanket tighter around him. "Well, you needn't be."

"You'll lose your job."

"No, I won't. It was only once, and I told Joyce to tell the captain I was sick."

"Joyce? She was here?"

"Yeah, she woke me up at some God forsaken hour. How did you know about this anyway?"

"Captain called your mother."

"Shit," he muttered. "I guess Joyce didn't tell him. Damn her." He pushed off the covers and stood, completely naked as he'd suspected. Xander felt the saliva gather in his mouth. Damn it, he was drooling. Sundar didn't seem to be in any hurry to cover up either. Why should he, with a body like that? Xander looked at the floor. "You should call your mother."

"I'm not five years old."

"I know, but she's worried and…I can't. I can't even form words. Can you please cover up?"

Sundar reached for his robe but it was too late. Xander was already hard as hell.

"Why didn't you go to work?"

"I didn't feel like it," he shrugged and walked out of the room.

I want your body. I want to touch you, I want to hold you. Damn, this is agony. Xander followed him. "Are you sick?"

"Yeah," he glared at him, "sick of all these damn questions." He began to fill the coffeemaker with water from the tap.

"Were you drunk last night?"

"Very," he said, searching for the coffee in the fridge.

"Does getting drunk help you to believe you don't want to fuck me anymore?"

He glanced at him, the coffee scoop in mid air. "Don't flatter yourself. I wasn't drinking because of you."

"You can look me in the eye right now and tell me that..."

The doorbell rang.

"Ah," he said with a smug smile, "saved by the bell."

Xander turned to see who was at the door as Sundar opened it. It was a tall, good looking guy in his late twenties. He looked like he might have been in some kind of an accident because he had a bandage on his head, and his face was bruised.

Sundar seemed surprised. "Mark?"

"I hope this isn't a bad time. I was in the neighbourhood. I figured you weren't going to call me so..."

"I appreciate what you did for me last night, Mark, but... Ah...come in."

"You're not going to hit me again, are you?" he lifted an eyebrow, a faint smile on his face.

"No. I'll try to control myself."

The guy called Mark was now eyeing Xander curiously.

"Oh yeah, Mark," Sundar introduced haphazardly, "Xander. Xander is my mother's boarder."

Ouch. Is that all I am? Jesus Christ.

Mark shook his hand. "Nice to meet you, Xander."

"You too."

"So, did Sunny tell you what happened last night?"

"No, I didn't," Sundar said sharply, "and he doesn't need to know either."

"I can leave," Xander said. "I'll just call your mom and get..."

"I don't need a babysitter, Xander," Sundar said, bringing his coffee cup to the table.

Xander nodded at him. "Fine. I'll let her know when I get back there. Glad you're all right." He eyed Mark. "And that you have a new friend." That was hard to say. "Bye," he said and barrelled through the front door. He took the stairs two at a time and raced to Sophia's car. So, Sundar was drunk last night and he was with that Mark guy. Things must have been pretty wild. Why'd he hit him? And what in hell was that guy coming around for? He still didn't understand why Sundar had played hooky from work. What if Sundar did accept his sexuality, and ended up falling for another guy? That would be unbearable. Xander got into Sophia's car and sat there. He had a few questions for this Mark guy and he wasn't leaving until he got the answers.

"He's sweet," Mark commented as he sat across from Sundar at the table, prepared to take a sip of the coffee. "He's in love with you, you know."

"No, he's not."

"Yeah, he is. You've fucked him; that I'd stake my life on. How many times was it?"

"That's none of your…"

"Ah, we had a deal. How many times did you make love to that poor, heartbroken bastard?"

"Twice. It was nothing. And he's not a heartbroken bastard."

"It might have been nothing to you, but it certainly was something to him." Mark studied him for a minute. "Did you read my card?"

"No."

"Here," he dug in his pocket, "take this one." He pushed it across the table at him.

Sundar sighed as he picked it up. "*Sexual Therapist: Acceptance and celebration of sexual diversity.*" He dropped it back on the table. "What does this have to do with me?"

"We help people come out of the closet and take pride in being gay. Sundar, I had to go through it. It almost killed me but now I'm fine, and I help others."

"You called me Sundar."

"It's your name, right?"

"Yes. But you always called me Sunny."

"You don't seem like a Sunny today. Come to the sessions."

"Sessions?"

"It will help you discover who you are, Sundar."

"I know who I am."

"You think you know. That young man who raced out of here all upset, he knows who you are when you're with him in bed. And that's who he needs you to be. I don't know if you love that guy, doesn't matter, there will be others. But you're going to be one lonely man if you continue to…"

The doorbell rang again. Sundar stood. "Sorry. It's Grand Central here today. We're going to have to end this little chat. Now, I promised to talk to you, and I did. So, am I off the hook now?"

"Not by a long shot."

Sundar sighed and walked to the door. It was Joyce. Shit. "Why didn't you tell the captain I called in sick?" he demanded before she had time to walk in the door.

"I'm not doing your dirty work," she snapped. "Anyway, I did tell him when I had a moment, and he wasn't happy about it. What in hell happened to you last night anyway?"

Mark was standing by the table. Sundar took a breath. "This is an old friend of mine from high school."

Mark came over and shook her hand. "Pleased to meet you. Well," he turned to Sundar, "guess I'll be off. We'll talk soon?"

Sundar didn't reply. He watched him go.

Joyce shut the door behind Mark. "What in hell happened to him? Looks like a cyclone hit him."

He didn't reply.

"What in hell is going on with you?"

"I drank too much last night, that's all."

"You got drunk and decided not to go to work!"

"Why didn't you tell the captain straight away? He called my mother for Christ's sake."

"Who was that guy who just left here? Was he in an accident?"

"Yeah, my fist met his face."

"What?"

He sighed. "You asked. How is your family?"

"Fine, okay, but Sunny — are you all right?"

He sunk down on the sofa. She came and sat beside him. He put his arm around her and hugged her close to him. "Sure."

"I want to meet your family. We'll go there for New Year's."

"Whatever you want," he said absently.

She kissed his neck. "I've missed you. Want to mess around?"

He kissed her mouth gently. "Later. I need to go to the precinct and smooth things over with the captain. And I don't know if I can have New Year's off."

"You'll either have New Year's Eve or Day. Ask nicely." She stretched out on the sofa.

"I'm going to take a shower."

"So, is he fucking you?" Xander asked Mark, holding his breath until he answered.

"I wish. No, don't worry. We just met up again, haven't seen him since high school, and I got ploughed. I wouldn't mind however. He's so hot."

"Yeah. So, why'd he hit you?"

"I told him something he didn't want to hear."

"Oh. Like?"

"Like he was in the closet."

"That would do it. Was there ever anything between you? Were you lovers?"

He grinned. "Stop worrying. I wish. I wanted him so badly back in high school but neither one of us was in touch with who we were. It never happened but God, I dreamed it over and over."

Xander moved the spoon around in his coffee cup for a few seconds then looked up at him. "This therapy stuff you do, does it work?"

"If the person wants it to. We can't drag 'em out of the closet kicking and screaming. We can only hold them up while they're struggling."

Xander studied him. He'd been nervous approaching this guy when he'd come out of Sundar's place, but as it turned out, Mark seemed glad that he'd waited. He'd invited him for coffee, and they'd made their way to a small café down the street.

"I know who you are," he told Mark suddenly. "Did you used to jerk off in front of Sundar in the locker room?" After he'd said it, he apologised.

He didn't seem embarrassed. "It's okay, and yeah, that was me. Sunny was so gorgeous, and a great football player too. I just couldn't reconcile the feelings I had. I guess I wanted him to make the first move because hey macho football players didn't fuck each other right? We'd play these games, him and I, get ourselves all hot and bothered. Mostly we showed off our bodies to each other and watched." He laughed. "Not so funny now. I went through hell, Xander. I drank, I did drugs, and I hit rock bottom before someone told me I had to accept myself. Eventually, I fell in love with someone who was worse than I was when it came to being in the closet. Now, it's no more closet guys for me."

"Sundar will never come out completely."

"I think you're wrong. Love will force him out."

"Love. You think?"

"Yeah. I do."

"He's a cop, you know. He has the kind of job that requires this image of macho…"

"It's not the job," Mark intercepted, shaking his head. "It's personal acceptance. If he accepts himself, so will others. I think he really cares about you, Xander. I can see it when he looks at you."

"Mark, I'm in love with him."

"Then don't give up on him," he reached across and took his hand. "He's struggling. Make him see that he needs you. Don't run from him, and don't let him hide from you. Get in his face at every opportunity. Remind him of his feelings."

"What then? I should just seduce him at any opportunity?"

Mark laughed. "That's the ticket. God, honey," he leaned across the table, "you can't tell me that would be too tough of an assignment, with a man who looks as good as Sundar does."

Xander sat back in his seat. "Sweetest job in the world, but I want more than just his body, Mark. I want his heart.

I want him to be proud to be my man. I don't want to meet him in dark alleys for the rest of our lives."

"That will come at the end if sees the light, you know that."

"How long is this going to take? And what if he doesn't, as you say, see the light?"

Mark stood up and put on his jacket. "There are no guarantees. Another thing, if he gets pissed," he rubbed his jaw, "duck 'cause he's got one hell of a mean right hook."

Xander laughed a little and thanked him.

"Here's my card. Call me anytime. See you."

Xander sat there staring at the card for a moment then he got up and left.

* * * *

Sundar took a taxi to go and get his car. When he arrived at the precinct, the captain was in a meeting and he had to wait over an hour to see him. "Roger," he said when he finally walked into his office, "I want to explain what happened...why I..."

"Close the door, Sundar, and take a seat."

Sundar sunk into the chair across from Roger Colts.

"Now before you say anything," the captain said, "I want you to know that I know all about last night."

"What?"

"You got drunk and hit a guy in the parking lot at the..."

"How in the hell did you..."

"The officers who took the call didn't tell me. There was a witness there at the bar who called me this morning, an off duty cop from another precinct."

Sundar muttered under his breath.

"He was concerned with your behaviour. It's a reflection on all of us. What is going on with you?"

"Nothing. I got drunk, okay? I made a mistake. You want my badge?" He stood.

"Calm down. Kingfisher. I don't want your badge. I want an explanation. You were lucky this time — the guy didn't press charges. You knew this man?"

"From high school. It was an old score and I told you, I was drunk. It's the holidays. Give me a break."

"You're a cop. You're not an ordinary man, Sunny. You have to set an example. For a civilian, what happened was explainable. For a detective who has sworn to serve and protect, it's not acceptable behaviour."

"So, you're going to reprimand me?"

"I need you. You're the best cop I got on the force."

Sundar raised an eyebrow.

"Is it Joyce?"

"What?"

"Don't play dumb, I know something is going on between the two of you. The way she looks at you, all doe eyed. It's against the rules, fraternization with other officers."

"I know."

"But you like to break the rules. Just be careful, Kingfisher, that you don't break one too many. Whatever is going on with you, fix it. I'm giving you three days do that."

"Three days?"

"On your own time, and it comes off your vacation total."

"No pay?"

The captain looked at him. "I could do worse and you know it. It's between you and me, off the books. To the others, it's a sick leave. You got it?"

"Yes sir," he said, standing. "I got it."

"Now, go home and work on it. And when you come back, I don't want to see it here at the office. And don't think of asking for New Year's. I want you back here on New Year's Day, working. Is that understood?"

Sundar nodded then left without another word. *What in fuck? He didn't want to see* what *here?* He came to work, did his job.

He left his car in the parking lot at the police station and took a long walk. He thought about Mark, and Xander, and Joyce. The three of them danced round and round in his head. By the time he returned to his car, he was drained, both emotionally and physically. He drove to his apartment, saw Joyce's car outside, and kept on driving.

Xander had gone home to give Sophia the message that Sundar was all right and then told her he was taking the bus back to his brother's and spending the New Year there. Sophia insisted on driving him home. "Over there beyond those mountains is where Clint's people are from," she told him as she drove. "The Tsalagi people are a proud people with a sad history. Do you know about the trail of tears?"

"The relocation of the Cherokee to Oklahoma. Yes. It was a tragedy. Many died."

"Yes, and they supported the United States against other tribes."

"It was a travesty, a not so pretty side of our history."

"A lot of that in our history," she muttered.

"Sundar doesn't seem very Cherokee."

"He's been denied his heritage. Clint won't even acknowledge his Indian heritage, although it's there for all to see. I used to take Sundar to see his grandfather when he was young, you know. He taught him to ride and rope, told him stories about his people. No one should ever be ashamed of who he is, ever. That's a travesty too."

Xander reached over and squeezed her hand. "You're right."

"You care a lot about my son, don't you, Xander?" She glanced at him.

"Yes. I guess you know that I'm…"

"Homosexual? They call it gay now. I don't think that my son is, well…so open-minded about that stuff. Is that the problem between you, he doesn't approve that you're, you know?"

"Kind of, yes."

"I'm sorry. Sundar will come around. And there will be someone out there for you."

It wasn't his place to tell her the real story. He just nodded.

"I don't think less of you because you're…isn't it gay now?" she reconfirmed.

"Yes. And thank you."

"I'm not sure what Clint would think of it so maybe we should keep that as our secret, okay?"

"Sure," he said, "no problem. It's too bad Clint can't embrace who he is."

"Yes," she said, "it is."

And too bad his son can't either.

"So our New Year's is ruined," Joyce announced.

Sundar sat on the sofa in front of the television, trying to concentrate on the hockey game. "Your New Year's isn't ruined, mine is."

"I thought we were going to your parents."

"Well, we're not."

"Don't you think you should be doing something more productive with your time than watching sports?"

"No."

"Sunny!" she protested.

"Would it hurt you once to call me by my name?" He kept his eyes on the television.

"It's a weird name."

He glanced at her. "Thanks."

She laughed. "Honey, come on. Let's go out. I don't have to work until midnight. I'd love to eat at that Italian place."

He sighed. "I'm supposed to be thinking."

"About what?"

"I'm not sure."

Joyce came and sat beside him. "Have you thought anymore about a date?"

"Date for?"

"You know what, our wedding?"

"Joyce," he sighed, looking at her. "Maybe you don't want to marry me."

"Why, because you lost your temper in a parking lot? That guy looked like a jerk anyway."

"He's not a...he's all right."

"If he's all right, why did you hit him?"

"I don't know. I was drunk. I messed up, okay? Let's not talk about it."

"Fine," she said, placing a hand on his thigh. "Let's go to bed then? You've been ignoring me lately."

She undid his zipper but damn it, he wasn't in the mood. But if he said no, what in hell did that mean? Wasn't every straight man supposed to want sex all the time?

He forced his head back on the sofa, let her play with his cock a few minutes. *Come on, get hard, get hard.* He'd never had any problems before.

His shirt was undone now and Joyce was kissing his chest. He had the suddenly urge to push her away. Her hand kept stroking his cock and all he was met with was frustration. *Faggot. Can't get it up for a woman. You're a faggot, Sundar.*

"Stop," he said, squeezing her hand.

She stood up, smiled at him, began to undress. "Come in the bedroom. Come and fuck me," she invited, taking off her bra and dangling it in her hand as she went.

He sighed and got up off the sofa. He took his cock in hand, stroked it. *Fuck me, Sundar, oh yeah, like that, on all fours. Fuck me.* "Xander," he whispered, his cock responded. He smiled to himself and made his way to the bedroom. *So what if I need a little help?*

Joyce lay naked on the bed, waiting. He stripped off his clothes and lay down beside her. "God, you're so hard and big," she cooed.

"Yeah," he smiled; kissing her lips gently then he pushed her over onto her stomach. "I'm going to take you from behind."

"You mean, anal?" She sounded disgusted.

"No, no, unless you want. Not anal," he pulled her up, playing with her large breasts. She enjoyed that. "Vaginally, only from behind. I can go deeper."

"Um, keep playing with my nipples like that," she invited. "And take me the way you want."

He closed his eyes. He saw Xander on his knees, felt his cock go into his ass. "Baby," he whispered, "God, I love your ass." He grunted as he went into her, pumping and pumping, wanting to come. Joyce screamed in orgasm as he stimulated her with his finger and kept pumping into her. He knew she wanted him to finish but he was still hard. "Damn it," he muttered, his hair wet against his forehead. He pulled out, turned her to face him and went into her again. It felt stilted, wooden even. She moaned under him and he pulled out, jerking himself into release and falling back on the pillows.

"That was good," she said, cuddling up beside him.

He was exhausted, unsatisfied, disgusted at himself as a man. If she thought all was normal, fine, but he knew it wasn't.

He spent the rest of the day frustrated. They went to dinner, she went to work, and Sundar bought a bottle at the liquor store and went home to drink it.

Xander's brother and his wife loved Sophia. She ended up staying for supper, and they had a great time. She said she'd come back and get him on the weekend. "She's a nice woman," Barbara told him after Sophia had left. She picked up the some dishes from the table and went into the kitchen.

Xander was about to give her a hand when Nathan stopped him. "Wait," he said. "We haven't had much time to talk."

Xander sat back down.

"How's it going?"

"I went to speak to the manager at the hotel. I'm all ready to begin after the holiday."

"You seem sad."

"Sad?"

"Xander, I know you. Why did you go and stay with the Kingfishers right away? Why didn't you stay here until after the holiday? If it's Barbara, I can talk to her. You're my brother and —"

"It's not Barbara."

"Is there someone?"

He swallowed. "You've never wanted to know before."

"You've never looked so depressed before. Even when you smile…you're not the same. Has he hurt you, cheated on you? Are you in love?"

He bit his lip. "Yes, I'm in love. And it's difficult to explain, that's all. It was a fluke how we met, and he's involved with a woman."

"Closet?"

Xander nodded.

"Find someone else. He's going to break your heart."

"I can't. I love him too much. I don't want to give up on him, Nathan. He's a good man."

"If he can't be true to himself…." Nathan put up his hand.

Nathan fell silent.

Xander had told him that he was boarding with Sundar's parents.

"Do you think it's a good idea, living with his parents?"

"Makes me feel close to him. I need to feel close to him." Tears sparked his eyes.

Nathan leaned over and placed his forehead against his. "You'll always have a home here."

"I know," Nathan said. "I know."

When the doorbell rang, Sundar almost didn't answer. He had passed out on the sofa with his half empty bottle of whisky, and he wasn't in the mood for company.

He checked the clock on the wall and groaned. It was almost midnight. "Joyce, did you forget something?" he mumbled.

When he opened it, he saw Mark standing there. "I haven't heard from you. You look like shit."

He walked in and closed the door. "It's late. What are you doing here?"

"I wanted to check on you. Drinking again?"

"It's not a crime, is it?"

"It is where you're concerned. You get mean. Where's Xander?"

"I have no idea. Why don't you go and find out?" Sundar staggered back to the sofa and sat down. The bottle was sitting beside him. "Want a drink?"

"No. I gave it up years ago. It will kill you."

"Um. So they say. How's the head?"

"Fine, no thanks to you." He took a seat in the chair across from him. "Why aren't you working?"

"Boss gave me an unpaid holiday for being a bad boy."

"Ah."

"But I get to work New Year's. Yeah!"

Mark laughed. "You sounded exactly like you did back in high school."

"Great."

"So how's your sex life?"

Sundar laughed.

"What?"

"How's yours?"

"Fine."

"Then why aren't you at home getting laid?"

"I'm single now."

"Oh, well there are plenty of gay bars."

"Visit any lately?"

"I don't go to those places."

"Tell me about how you and Xander met?"

"It was mistaken identity. I thought he was the kid I was looking for."

"And so you fucked him?"

"No," he protested. "It just happened."

"And it just happened… twice?"

"Something like that."

"And if there was no homophobia in this world, would you be with Xander?"

"Stupid question."

"Let me put it this way, if being gay made you more of a man in the eyes of people around you, would Xander be in your bed right now?"

"I think you should go and find someone to fuck you, Mark," he sighed.

"Want to?" he invited.

"What?"

"Fuck me? You want to?" He stood up. "Xander would hate me for this, but I think it's a long time coming. We should have done it back in high school."

Sundar swallowed hard. He looked at him. *Yeah. Oh yeah. He wanted to. He wanted to feel his hard body against his, bury his cock into his ass. Stop this ache inside of him that still felt tender and unsatisfied.* " No." He turned his face away.

"You're lying." Mark came and stood in front of him. He knocked his legs apart with his knees.

Sundar looked up at him.

Mark undid his pants.

"More games?"

"No games this time," he said.

Chapter Seven

Xander's first day at the hotel was hectic. He didn't know the routine, didn't know where anything was, but the staff was patient with him. The manager, Rob Curtain, started him off as a bellhop. "You have to learn the business from the bottom up."

It was a little disappointing but he knew going in that to learn the business, you had to know every job inside out. At the end of the day, his back ached, and he had a wicked headache.

"It will be better tomorrow," Rob told him with a smile.

He was a handsome, personable man, and Xander noticed him looking at him often. He wondered if Rob was gay. But then, it didn't matter, his heart belonged to someone else.

Xander was surprised to see Joyce at the house that evening when he arrived. She was huddled at the table with Sophia, and she'd been crying. "Joyce?" he said in surprise. "What are you doing here?"

"I needed to talk to Sunny's mother," she said, wiping her eyes.

"Sundar is acting strange," Sophia pursed her lips.

"He wouldn't open the door for me. He had someone in his apartment. I think it's that strange man who had the accident."

"What strange man?" Sophia asked.

"Mark?" Xander echoed.

"Yeah, there's something really weird about him. I don't like him."

Maybe Mark was counselling Sundar, trying to help him to…or maybe he was fucking him. That bastard!

"You know how men are," Sundar's mother was saying. "I'm sure it's nothing."

"I just don't understand it. And he's really taking his time about choosing a date for the wedding." She started to cry again.

Sundar's father walked into the kitchen now. He looked at Xander. "They still at this?"

"Be sensitive," Sophia clicked her tongue. "Your son is being a typical man, insensitive and…"

"My son now?" Clint Kingfisher chuckled. "Oh okay, I'm outside with the horses. Carry on, ladies."

Sophia muttered something under her breath.

"You go and talk to him," Joyce said suddenly, looking at Xander. "Maybe he'll let you in."

"I, ah…don't think…I'm the best…really…"

"Go, Xander, take the car. Please?" Sophia pleaded.

Xander nodded. "Okay." He leaned down and kissed her cheek. "Don't worry."

Mark dropped back onto the bed with a sigh of pleasure. He wiped his hand over his sweaty chest and laughed out loud.

Sundar watched him for a moment then stood up and walked to the bathroom. Sex with Mark satisfied that spot down deep that was difficult to touch sometimes, and yet, there were no complicated feelings associated with it. Hard, raunchy sex, rocking his soul, scraping down to that core, and there was no touchy feely bullshit.

"God, that was good," Mark declared as Sundar came back out of the bathroom. "You fuck like a real champion."

"Guess I missed my calling."

"What are you going to do about Joyce?"

He shrugged, pulled on his pants. "Marry her, I guess."

"Marry her, you guess?" he said up and stared at him. "Sundar, come on. She deserves more than that. You're being an insensitive prick."

"Thanks," he said, picking up his shirt.

"You love Xander."

"How in the hell do you know who I love?"

"Because. It's easy here with me, fucking. You feel nothing, but it's got to end."

"Why?" Sundar glanced at him. "I'm perfectly happy with it."

Mark gave him a faint smile and swung his legs over the side of bed. "I'm falling in love. And you don't want that."

"Fuck." Sundar shook his head. "Why do you have to ruin it?"

"I can't help my feelings. I've always been attracted to you, and I knew you needed me. I didn't intend it to go on all this time. Five times we've been together, and your head is still in another place. You're not going to fall for me, and you're going to deny yourself the one man you love because then it becomes too damn real."

"Back to the psycho babble."

"You need to hear this. You'll lose him, and you'll hurt Joyce badly. Those two people are in love with you, and personally, I don't want to join the 'in love with Sundar fan club', okay? So, guess you'll have to start sleeping with strangers."

"Mark," he began but then the doorbell rang "Shit."

"Probably Joyce again. You should let her in this time."

Sundar watched Mark put on his pants. "Get dressed."

"Don't worry. I won't tell her what's been going on."

Sundar left the room. He closed the door to and then called out, "I'm coming, Joyce."

When he opened it, he was almost relieved to see Xander standing there — better him than Joyce right now. "What is it?"

"Joyce is crying her eyes out."

"And you're her advocate right now? I'll deal with Joyce."

"Are you fucking Mark?"

The question floored him for a moment.

Xander took the opportunity to come inside and close the door behind him. "Mark said he'd help me, and here he is…" He trailed off as Mark made an appearance.

"It's over," Mark told Xander, picking up his jacket. "You may want to spend your life in love with a man you can never have, but I don't. I've been there before, so I'm getting out before it's too late." He walked over and placed a hand on Xander's shoulder.

Xander knocked it off.

"I'm sorry I betrayed you." He looked at Sundar. "I couldn't seem to help myself. But you can have him, good luck. He's looking for a fuck without emotion, guess that lets you out, buddy. And I'm out of here."

Xander was staring at Sundar as the door slammed shut.

"Don't look at me like that." He turned away, walked back to the bedroom and began stripping the bed.

"I understood you trying to avoid me, trying to deny who you are, but you fucked Mark? How many times?"

Sundar could hear the pain in Xander's voice. It was too much. "Look, just go. I don't want you here. Go!"

There was silence.

Sundar turned around. "Please, Xander."

"I love you," he whispered. "I'll always love you, Sundar, but you're tearing me apart. Don't marry Joyce. You'll tear her apart as well."

He nodded. "Okay."

"I'm going to say something I thought I would never say." He was trembling.

Sundar squeezed his eyes shut. He wanted to hold him but that would have been a bad move. "Say it."

"Don't touch me anymore. If I'm alone in a room, stay out. Stay away from me as much as possible, and I'll do the same. Okay?" His eyes were filled with tears.

Sundar swallowed and nodded.

"Thank you," Xander managed. He turned and left the bedroom.

Sundar sat down on the bed and clutched the sheet in his fist. The front door banged shut. He swallowed the lump in his throat. It was for the best. He couldn't hide who he was with Joyce either. Xander and Mark were right about that. His best bet was to just soothe the ache when he had the opportunity without emotional involvement of any kind. Mark had been ideal, hot sex without any attachment. But that was over. Mark had to go and get personal. If he was careful, male prostitutes would do, but he knew it wasn't smart. He was a cop for one thing and vulnerable to blackmail, not to mention sexually transmitted diseases.

"Fuck!" he yelled, throwing the sheet aside. It was time for a drink.

* * * *

It was tough to hide how miserable he was and by midweek, his boss was asking him if he was all right.

"Fine," he said, forcing a smile. "Why? Is something wrong?"

"I know playing bellhop is not that exciting, but..."

"I'm not complaining," he said. "I know it's important. I'm sure you did it too."

"Yeah, I did. Can't say I miss it." He grinned. "Hey listen, if you're not busy tonight, how about we do dinner and ah..." he lowered his voice, as the desk clerk came back to the front, "talk more about your career. You can say no. This isn't sexual harassment or anything."

Xander sucked in some breath. Why not? He was good looking, nice, and obviously not ashamed of his feelings. "I'd love to," he said.

At four o'clock he called Sophia to say he had been invited out to dinner, and not to plan anything for him.

"How nice," she said. "A nice boy?"

He laughed a little at the word 'boy'. My boss actually, business dinner."

"Is he hot?"

"Sophia!"

She laughed. "I'm sorry, just everything is so blah. I haven't heard back from Joyce or Sundar."

"I'm sure they'll work it out," he said stiffly. "Talk to you later."

He didn't want to hear about Sundar anymore.

Dinner was pleasant. Rob was charming and talkative, and by the end of the evening, Rob made it quite clear that he was interested in knowing Xander better. In the car, Rob leaned over to kiss him goodbye and Xander froze. He felt like a fool, apologised and then leaned in to give Rob a quick kiss as an apology. "I'm sorry," Rob said. "I was out of line. I shouldn't have…"

"No," Xander said. "It's not you. It's me, really. I…" He sighed. "I was involved with…well…not really. Anyway, it's over. Rob, I like you," he said.

"I'm a patient man, Xander. Don't worry about it."

Xander smiled and got out of the car. "Thanks for dinner. See you tomorrow?"

Rob lifted a hand and drove away.

* * * *

Sundar was on the phone each time Joyce came by his desk. He had a lead in a case he'd been working on for a few months, and he was tracking down the people he needed to interview again. He was glad of the diversion. He'd been putting off talking to her.

He was picking up his car keys and putting on his coat when she appeared in front of his desk again. He concentrated on fiddling in his pocket. He felt guilty. What else could he feel? "I'm sorry, Joyce," he said, glancing up, "I've got to be somewhere."

"We need to talk." She crossed her arms. "What did I do?"

"You didn't do anything," he lowered his voice. "And this is not the time. The captain already knows about us, and he's busting my ass." He came around the desk.

"Is there an 'us'?"

The detectives hanging around the water cooler were looking at them.

"I promise we'll talk, okay, but not now."

He brushed past her. Joyce followed him out the door and down the hallway. "Tonight. We talk tonight, Sunny. I can't stand the suspense anymore."

He turned and glanced at her, nodded then left.

* * * *

It had been almost three weeks now since Xander had started his work placement at the hotel. Rob gave his supervisor at the school a very good review, and Xander was put on the front desk.

He and Rob had been out three times and they really got along well. Rob hadn't tried to kiss him again and Xander was wondering whether he should try it again.

"If you have to think about it," Mike told him on the phone, "it's because there's no passion."

"Don't say that. Rob is good looking, successful, sexy, and I'm sure that…" He wanted so much to fall in love with him.

"But you need chemistry."

"Chemistry? Ha, where in hell has that ever gotten me? I had tons of chemistry with Sundar, and look where that got me."

"How is Sundar?"

"I have no idea. He's not around. He avoids me like the plague, and his mother is upset that he doesn't visit."

"He's a closeted freak. Have you heard from David?"

"Not in awhile."

"He's got a new boyfriend, you know."

Xander sighed. "We weren't a couple or anything. I hope he's happy."

"Want to see a movie this weekend?"

"Not this weekend, I'm beat. Call me next week, okay?"

They said their goodbyes and hung up. Xander lay back on the bed and fell asleep.

The phone woke him up a half hour later. It was Rob. "Want to go for a drive?" he asked. "I know you're tired but we won't stay out late."

"Sure," Xander said. Tonight was the night that he and Rob would become lovers. All he had to do was take the plunge. He'd be in love, he was sure. Eventually.

* * * *

Sundar knew it was time he went to see his mother. She'd left several messages on his machine. He needed to tell her about Joyce and him. He drove up into the driveway and waited, looking up to see if there was a light on in his old room. If Xander was in, he'd just have to deal.

He sighed, and got out, walking up to the door slowly, noticing that the house was quiet. He turned the handle and walked in. They never locked their door.

"Mom, Dad?"

His mother came running down the hallway. "Sundar!"

He enfolded her in a bear hug. No matter how badly he behaved as a child, she'd always forgiven him. This time he held on a little longer, pressing his cheek against hers.

"What's the matter?" she asked.

"Nothing," he replied, releasing her. "Where is...ah, everyone?" And suddenly he felt desperate to see Xander, just to say hello.

"It's your dad's poker night, you know that," she said, heading back into the kitchen. He followed. "Tea?"

"No thanks." He wanted a drink.

"Sit down. Where in hell have you been?"

He sat across from her, shrugged out of his coat. "Busy at work and…Mom, Joyce and I are not together anymore. Thought you should know."

"Don't blame that girl for leaving, the way you treated her."

"She didn't leave me. We decided to split, that's all."

"Must not be comfortable at work."

"She put in for a transfer."

His mother reached over and covered his hand with hers. "I don't want to see you end up alone."

He nodded. "Don't worry about me."

"My big, tough son," she muttered. "You're your father all over."

"No, I'm not like him." He shook his head.

"Yes," she nodded, "you are."

"How are you?" He didn't want to talk about that anymore.

"Fine. And Xander is fine. Son, you should be more tolerant of people who are different. You're not a racist."

"What are you talking about?" He wrinkled up his face.

"Xander is gay but that doesn't make him a bad person. Why can't you be friends?"

"Did he tell you I was homophobic?"

"Not in so many words, but I gather that's why you don't like him."

"I never said I didn't like him. We just don't have anything in common, and I don't give a shit if he's gay."

"He's found a nice guy now. I'm happy for him. Now, if only you…"

"What?" Everything seemed to stand still. "What did you say about Xander?"

"Just that he's dating his boss at the hotel. He's such a nice man, came and picked him up tonight, came in and said hello. He's tall and handsome, just like a fairy tale, pardon the pun." She giggled. "You know, I've known that man for a few years and I would have never guessed that he…"

His mother kept talking but Sundar could no longer hear her. Xander was seeing someone. "Is he in love with this guy?" He met his mother's gaze.

"Heavens, I don't know anything about that sort of thing. They just started seeing each other, but he seems happy."

What should he care? "You know what?" He stood. "Fuck Xander, and fuck the hotel manager too."

"Sundar, what are you getting so hostile for?"

"I've got to go," he said. "See you, Mom, say hello to Dad for me."

He swung out of the driveway, his foot heavy on the gas. He had no right to be upset. Xander wasn't his. He'd never be his. He had the right to be happy. He checked the clock on the dashboard. It was only nine. He had a few hours before he had to be to work. He took the next exit and drove to a place on the far side of town, a clandestine club where men could purchase whatever sexual entertainment they wanted. He needed some sexual release, along with a few drinks; he'd be ready to face the night.

"It's all right," Rob told Xander. "You're just not ready."

Xander turned around on the bed, his gaze running over Rob's naked body. "It's not because you're not an attractive man, Rob."

"Look, you gave me one hell of a blowjob. I'm just sorry you won't let me return the favour, and if you don't want to fuck, that's okay. Some men are just not into that and…"

"Stop being so damn nice."

"It's easy to be nice to you, Xander."

Tears rolled down his cheeks. He brushed them away. Oh, he'd tried so hard to wipe him from his mind, and he just wouldn't go away. "I'm in love with another man," he said.

Rob sat up. "I see."

"No, you don't see. We will never be together. He's in the closet, and he intends to stay there. So I should forget him and move on, and I'm trying but…"

Rob pulled Xander into his arms. He held him for a few minutes. "Easier said than done, right?"

Xander nodded. "I'm sorry, Rob."

"That's okay, Xander. Like I say, I'm a patient man, and you're worth it."

Xander kissed him passionately on the mouth and Rob kissed him back. They fell together on the bed, and Xander moved his hands over Rob's chest and stomach. *Sundar. If only he were you.*

"One hundred dollars and all the booze you can hold."

Sundar took five twenties out of his wallet and tossed them on the counter. "I want to fuck, no touchy feely stuff, and with someone who can take it."

"You're definitely a rider," he looked him up and down. "I can always tell. Looking for a bit of the rough tonight, eh?"

"I don't need your comments, just give me a tight ass, and leave me alone with him."

He grinned. "I like your style. Okay, well, I have two in mind. Go sit at a table, have a few drinks and I'll send them over."

"I have two hours then I'm gone, so do it quick."

He smiled at him with decaying front teeth. It was quite disgusting. He hoped the guy he sent to him knew something about oral hygiene. Oh well, he didn't intend on kissing the guy anyway.

He walked over to one of the tables and sat down. There was a glass of whisky waiting for him. He downed it, wiped his mouth on the back of his hand and waited. The place was dark and filled with men. On the stage, a naked guy was making love to a steel post. He wasn't particularly attractive.

Sundar signalled the waiter and drank down another glass of whisky. When a hand touched his forearm, he was more than ready. "Hello baby, why, aren't you something?" the young man drawled. He was wearing a pair of faded jeans and nothing else. He looked like he'd just got done fucking some other guy.

"Assembly line fucking," Sundar laughed to himself.

"What's that?" He reached out, pushed back a piece of stray hair.

"Nothing," Sundar muttered.

"What's your name?"

"Does it matter? Call me anything you want."

"Come with me."

"You know what I want?"

"Yeah, you want to fuck the shit out of me, and baby," he dragged him by the collar, "when a man looks as good as you, I'm more than willing to let him do it."

Xander sat quietly with Rob in the front seat of his car. Rob held his hand, and they listened to the radio. "I should go in," he said, looking at the house.

"I'm sorry," he said.

"You have nothing to be sorry for. It was me who couldn't…you know."

"Can we try it again?"

The answer was probably no. Rob was a great guy but he didn't turn him on in bed. It was that simple. "We'll see," he said with a smile. He didn't want to hurt his feelings. He checked the clock on the dash. It was eleven thirty and he was tired, glad to be able to sleep in tomorrow. "I think I'll go in," he repeated, leaning over to give him a kiss.

When the car came careening into the yard, Xander was just about to get out. If he had of, the car probably would have hit him. It came to a stop right beside Rob's car.

"What the hell?" Rob growled.

Xander peered out the window and opened the door. He saw Sundar make an attempt to get out of his vehicle. He was obviously loaded. "Sundar?"

"There he is," Sundar slurred, leaning against his car. "There he is with his new boy toy."

Xander turned and looked at Rob through the window. "It's okay, Rob, I'll handle this."

"I'm not leaving you," Rob said, making an attempt to get out of his car.

"No," Xander insisted, coming around and pushing the door closed. "It's okay, please. It's better you leave."

"Is this the jerk that is in the closet?" Rob demanded.

Sundar moved around the car. "What did you say?"

"No, Sundar," Xander told him, pushing him back. "Rob, leave now. Sundar, you'll be in trouble again. Think about this. Rob, please, just go. I'll be fine."

"Yeah, I'll take care of him," Sundar muttered.

"You call me if you have trouble," Rob said warily, turned the key in the ignition.

"I will. Please go. I'll see you Monday."

Sundar stood there swaying a little in front of a huge maple tree. The car drove slowly out of the yard.

"You just made an idiot out of yourself," Xander accused. "What in hell are you doing driving in that state? Where have you been?"

"Fucking," he announced. "I fucked this guy for an hour, punished his ass something wicked. Cost me a hundred dollars, booze was included." He laughed.

Xander bit his lip. "Is that supposed to punish me for something?"

"No."

"What are you doing here?"

"I wanted to introduce...wanted to meet the new boyfriend. What happened to the freak with the studs?"

"David was just a friend."

"Oh."

"What do you want, Sundar? You said you didn't want to see me anymore."

"I don't."

"Yet you're here. Come inside and sleep it off."

"With you?" The voice was soft suddenly, almost plaintive.

"Stop this, Sundar, you don't want me."

"Yes, I do," he replied, "and that's the problem."

Xander wanted to hold him but he held back. "I'm going inside."

"I'm leaving. Do you love him?"

Xander had his back turned. He didn't look at him. "No. Does it really matter?"

"I suppose not."

Xander forced himself to keep walking. "I'm not going to allow you to put my heart in a blender anymore. Fuck who you want," God, but that hurt, "and I'll do the same."

"Is he good?"

Xander moved closer to the door.

"Is he good?" Sundar shouted.

"He's fantastic," Xander replied, "better than you ever were. Happy?"

Sundar didn't reply. He headed to his car.

Xander watched him. He couldn't let him drive like that. If something happened to him, he'd never be able to bear it. He turned and ran to him. "Don't." He grabbed Sundar's arm.

Sundar looked at him. "Kiss me," he whispered. "I've missed you so much."

For a moment, Xander thought Sundar was going to cry, but he didn't. He wanted to kiss him but he held back.

"I can't let you drive. Give me your keys."

He threw out his arms. "Find them."

"I can't do this, please."

"Find them," he insisted, meeting his eyes. "Come on, touch me."

Xander moved his hands over his ribcage and searched his pockets, trying not to melt against him as he did. "The keys aren't there," Xander accused.

Sundar pointed to the ignition.

"Very funny."

"Felt fine," he grinned, opened the door. "Now, go dream about that manager who's such a great lover and leave me alone."

Xander tried to grab his arm but he was already in the driver's seat. He struggled with him but he knew that Sundar would win. He watched him drive off in fear; sure he was going to kill someone or himself. "What do you want from me?" he cried out.

Sophia was at the door when he walked up the path. "Was that Sundar? What's going on?"

He didn't have the heart to tell her that her son was loaded, and that he was so tormented, he was doing anything he could to kill the pain.

"Can I borrow the car?" he asked her.

"Now?"

"Please, it's important."

"Sure, go ahead," she said, watching him curiously. "Had Sundar been drinking?"

"A little."

She handed him the keys. "He acted quite violently tonight when I told him about Rob."

"You told him about Rob and me?"

"I mentioned only that you'd met a nice young man and you seemed happy."

"Damn."

"Did I do something wrong?"

"No, it's okay." He raced down to her car and got in, hoping the hell he could find Sundar before he did something stupid.

Sundar arrived at the police station but didn't stop. Instead, he kept on driving. There was no point showing up for work in this state. He'd get fired. He wasn't sure where he was going until he turned down a long unpaved road which wound around the river flowing towards the mountains. It was still dark when he pulled the car to a stop. He could see the house across the field and the large corral where the palomino horses grazed. It was cold and the wind whipped his hair around his face. "*dv ge `si-di `quenv `sv i*," he said. "I'm going home now."

He got back into his car and slept. When he woke up, his mouth felt like sawdust and he had a wicked headache. He left the car behind and began to walk across the field, and memories of his grandfather with his long flowing hair flooded over him. The pain dug into his temples. He heard his grandfather's voice. *Sundar, I will teach all that you should know, and one day you will return here as a man to seek answers. And you will find what you seek.*

When he got closer to the corral, the horses came to greet him and he stood there, rubbing his forehead against a grey mare.

The voice that spoke from behind him suddenly was deep and sharp. "What are you doing on my land?"

Slowly he turned around to see a man who looked much like his father, only older. He held a shotgun in his hand, his long grey streaked hair tied back at the neck. *Running Creek.*

Before Sundar could speak, the man lowered the gun. "Sundar, I knew you'd come."

"You recognise me?" He took a step forward.

"Of course. Blood always knows blood. You are welcome here."

"I remember coming here as a boy."

"Yes, we used to race the horses in the field. My father told me that one day you'd be back."

Sundar swallowed. "Yes."

"You can stay?"

"For a few days…if that's okay."

"Stay as long as you like. Come on in the house."

He couldn't find Sundar anywhere and right before morning, he gave up.

When he got to the house, Clint walked in the front door, holding a screwdriver in his hand. "Oh, hey there, kid," he said.

"Mr. Kingfisher," he nodded. "Any news from Sundar?"

"Why? What happened?"

"He showed up here drunk last night. I don't think he went to work."

"My son went off on his own, that's all. He's got a wild streak in him that boy. No cause for panic, he's not dead in the river somewhere." He shook his head. "I know Sundar. He can take care of himself."

Xander called the only person he knew might be able to help, even if he wasn't very happy with went on between him and Sundar. Xander hunted for the card Mark had given him. He found it in the pocket of his jacket. He stared at it a minute then dialled the number. "Mark, it's Xander. Look, I know about you and Sundar, but right now, that doesn't matter. I'm afraid he's done something to himself or…please, can we talk?"

"Where is Sundar now?"

"Gone. I'm worried."

"Gone? Like disappeared gone?"

"Kind of."

"Come down to the centre and we'll talk. He's probably fine."

"I'll be there soon," he said and hung up.

"You've put some meat on your bones since I last saw you, Sundar," his uncle told him as he handed him some coffee.

Sundar nodded.

They sat around an old wood stove in the kitchen. Nothing had changed since the last time he'd been here. The carpet was the same faded fabric. The walls were still yellow with cigarette smoke. The tin cup that contained his coffee was dented and chipped, and he remembered his grandfather drinking out of that cup.

He sipped the coffee quietly, feeling comforted somehow by it all.

"You look like shit."

"I have a drinking problem."

He didn't comment on that. "Hear you're a big city dick in Raleigh now," his uncle mentioned. "How's that working for you?"

"I like my job but if I keep on this way, I'm going to lose it."

He nodded. "Man's got to like what he does. You got to value that. How's Indra?"

"Indra?"

"My little brother?"

"That's his name, Indra?"

"You don't know your own father's name?"

"He always goes by Clint. I don't know my father very well."

"He doesn't know himself very well, so how can his son know him? Indra means God of rain and thunder," his uncle put down his cup. "On the night your father was born, there was a terrible storm. And as he grew up, we knew the name suited him. He was angry, like the sky when it opens up, angry at the world, angry at his family because he wanted to be someone he wasn't. He cut all ties with our parents, this land. And he thinks it makes him one of them, but he will never be able to cut out his own heart." He paused. "And you can't cut out your heart either, Sundar, so whatever it is that brought you home, you've got to face it."

"When I was a boy, grandfather showed me the sweat lodge. He said that when a man was lost, he could find himself there."

His uncle eyed him. "The lodge will purify, reveal the inner truth. Are you truly prepared to meet the truth, Sundar? If you're not ready, it will make things worse."

Sundar considered that. "I don't know if I'm ready but I know I have to do this. I feel myself slipping away little by little."

"Then we must prepare," his uncle stood.

"Prepare?" Sundar looked up at him.

"You must fast for twenty four hours before the sweat. I need to bring in lava rocks. You will be alone for the sweat, but I will bring you water. We will smoke the pipe before you go in. It will prepare your mind."

The centre Mark ran turned out to be three modest-sized rooms, with a computer, phone and fax machine. A dark haired woman put down the phone and greeted Xander when he walked in. "I'm looking for Mark," he said. "He told me to meet him here."

"Go on in," she said. "He's in his office."

Xander walked down the narrow corridor and spotted Mark sitting at his desk, staring at a computer screen. "Xander," he said, looking up. "Come in, sit down. Coffee?"

"No." He plunked down into the rather battered looking office chair. "Sundar has disappeared. I'm worried that it's because of me."

"He didn't show up at work?"

"No. His car wasn't parked at the precinct, and he was too drunk anyway. Mark, I'm afraid he's fucking up, and that it's my fault." He pushed a hand through his hair. "I couldn't bear it if I screwed up his career. Maybe I made a mistake taking a room at his parents' house."

"You can't blame yourself for his actions. Maybe he wanted to be alone. He's not a boy."

"I know that. I'm seeing someone else. Last night he showed up drunk in the yard where we were, and made a scene."

"He's in love with you." Mark looked away for a minute. "That's the reason he was fucking me. He felt nothing for me."

"I'd like to say that I'm sorry, Mark, but…"

"I don't expect you to. What happened with Joyce?"

"I don't know." He looked at him. "I'm sure it's over."

"He's going through hell. I saw it in his face. What can I do?"

"Be there for him if he needs you. I'll keep a look out for him. If I hear of anything, I'll let you know. I'm sure he's fine."

The floor was dirt, the tent round, and his uncle had covered the top of it with heavy wool blankets. The lava rocks had been sizzling for a few hours when his uncle told him to remove all his clothes and crawl inside.

Running Creek came inside as well, still fully dressed. He held a lit peace pipe in his hand. They sat across from each other and his uncle chanted some words that Sundar didn't quite understand. He took a long drag on the pipe then handed it to Sundar. After several drags on the pipe, his uncle rose and left the tent.

Everything seemed to spin. Sundar lay back and closed his eyes. *Please...help me. Take this ache away. Make me whole. Heal me.*

When Xander walked into the house, he heard two female voices talking at the kitchen table. He wished he could have avoided them but he had no choice but to walk in. He saw Sophia and Joyce, huddled over coffee cups, their brows furrowed with anxious worry. The conversation sounded almost manic.

"Xander," Sophia said, as if relieved to see him. "Any luck? Did you go looking for Sundar?"

"I just went to talk to a friend of his, to see if he'd seen him." *What was she doing here?*

"Where would he go?" Joyce spoke up. "Why would he just take off without letting anyone know? He is going to get suspended again. He didn't show up for work."

"He didn't?" Xander echoed.

"No. And he's not answering his cell phone," she sniffed, grabbing a tissue from the box on the table. "Why would he just turn it off?"

"I'm sure he's fine," Xander muttered. "Maybe he needs time alone to think."

"Think about what?" she demanded. "He's made it clear where we stand. He wants me out of his way. I'm being transferred next month."

"He'll change his mind," Sophia rubbed Joyce's shoulder.

"Let's hope he doesn't," Xander said.

Joyce glared at him. "What does that mean?"

"Xander," Sophia clicked her tongue.

Xander looked at his feet. *Shut up, Xander.*

"He's a cop, for Christ's sake," Clint bellowed, suddenly walking into the kitchen. "If you ladies would stop your fretting, it would be a good thing. Sundar didn't go out and shoot himself in the foot."

"You're not worried in the least?" Sophia accused.

Clint took some juice out of the fridge. "Nope. You'll hear something in a few days." He poured the juice and left the kitchen with it.

"Clint's right," Xander said, wanting to escape the kitchen before Joyce could pounce on him. She looked like she wanted to. "Sundar can take care of himself."

"I'm sorry about you two," Sophia said to Joyce. "Marriage would have been good for Sundar," Sophia looked at Xander. "Would have taken the wild out of him."

"I'm not giving up on him," Joyce announced.

Xander held his tongue. He excused himself and left the kitchen.

Are you a faggot, Sunny? Do you want to suck my cock? All that pussy you're getting from the cheerleaders doesn't do anything for you, does it?

Mark?

Sundar looked around him. He was alone. The sweat ran down his forehead and into his eyes. His chest, his stomach and his thighs were coated with it. Someone put some cool liquid to his lips and he swallowed then he was alone again. "Mark? Damn you! This is your fault. I'm not a faggot. I'm not. Stop it, stop…stop….

Sundar? Sundar, baby. I love your cock. I love the way you fuck me. Fuck me like that again. Please baby…please….

Xander?

He licked his lips, moaned. He reached down and wrapped his fist around his cock. *Hard. I'm so hard. Suck it. Suck my cock. Make it go away. Go away, Xander….get out of head…Goooooooooo!*

"Joyce? Save me." He whispered aloud. He opened his eyes. Directly above him Joyce floated, her hair flowing out behind her, her body erotically spread, naked, inviting. Her face changed, body parts appeared and disappeared. *Xander.*

The image disappeared again and he licked his dry lips. *Be true to yourself, my grandson. Be true. Be the man you were meant to be. Embrace your nature. Don't be like your father. Don't ever forget who you are.*

He was riding now on top of one of his grandfather's horses. His face was painted, his hair longer, flying out behind him as he rode. He wore only buckskin. His limbs were gloriously naked. He was free. Nothing around him but nature, rolling waterfalls, mountains and there, in the distance, someone waited for him. He rode and rode but he never reached the end. Cool water touched his lips again and he swallowed, falling into a dream-like state. Sleep. He wanted to sleep but his dozing was filled with images. A wolf with yellow eyes watched him carefully. He reached out to mist, nothing. There was nothing.

He hadn't had much sleep and the sun was cutting into his eyes something fierce as he drove. He wasn't sure if he was doing the right thing, but Clint's dream had propelled him forward. He'd had no choice.

The tall man who met him in the yard had a steady grip on a shot gun. He stared at him, demanding Xander introduce himself.

Xander slowly got out of Sophia Kingfisher's car, his hands up. A snarling German Shepherd snapped around his legs.

"Are you Running Creek?" Xander asked, warily looking at the salivating canine.

"King, heal!" he muttered and the dog went to lay at the big man's feet. "Yep. That's me. Who wants to know?"

"Clint Kingfisher sent me."

He narrowed his eyes.

"He woke me up in the middle of the night. Said he had a dream about Sundar, that he was here, and he wanted me to go to him, check and see if he was alright."

The big man lowered the gun. "And who are you?"

"My name is Xander. I'm boarding with the Kingfishers right now. I'm a…friend of Sundar's."

"He's here and he's fine. Tell my brother he needn't worry."

"Is he all right?"

Running Creek turned and pointed to a tent in the distance. Xander could see the smoke rising from the top. "He's in there with his spirit guide, looking for vision."

Xander swallowed. *Sundar was in a sweat lodge.* "Is he all right in there?"

"I was just about to go and pull him out actually. It's been over eight hours."

"Is it dangerous?"

"It can be if one doesn't know what they're doing. I've been making sure he has enough water. He's not dehydrated, but he's probably exhausted."

"Can I go in? I want to see him."

Running Creek seemed to be observing him closely. "Are you the reason he's in there?"

Xander entwined his hands together. "Maybe."

The bigger man nodded. "He's finished. You might as well go in."

Xander began walking towards the tent. "I need to talk to him alone."

The bigger man followed. "He won't be in much mood to talk. It's hot in there," he warned, "so don't stay in there long. Here, he'll need these." He handed him a water bottle and a blanket.

Xander took them, opened the flap and ducked inside. He caught his breath when he saw Sundar stretched out on the dirt floor. His flesh was slick with sweat and his cock was erect. Xander went to his knees and crawled over to him. He lifted his head and held the water to his lips. "Sundar? Are you all right?"

Sundar moaned slightly, accepted some of the water, coughed a bit and opened his eyes. He looked at him but he didn't seem to see him.

"Sundar, baby," he whispered, pressing his lips against his wet hair. "Baby. I didn't know where you went and..."

"Are you real?"

"Yes, I'm real." Xander ran a hand over Sundar's chest to his stomach and then took his erection in his hand. He squeezed it gently, kissing Sundar's dry lips at the same time. "Let me show you."

Sundar raised his hips higher, pushing his erection into Xander's hand. He moaned deeply in his chest. "Yes, yes," he whispered. "It's a dream."

Xander quickly removed his shirt and threw it aside then he unzipped his jeans and pushed them down along with his underwear. "It's not a dream," he whispered, continuing to stroke Sundar's cock. He discarded his pants and straddled Sundar's hips, his legs spread, knees on either side. "I need you inside of me. I need you to fuck me. It's okay. You don't need to do anything. I'll do everything."

He positioned Sundar's sweat-soaked cock under him and began to slowly descend on it until he felt his ass being penetrated by its hardness. He gritted his teeth. It hurt some without lubricant, but the pain only reminded him of how much he loved this man. "Baby, Sundar, I love you."

Xander swallowed Sundar's cock with his body then slowly began to move from side to side, up and down.

Sundar picked up his head and gasped with pleasure. "Um, yeah…oh yeah." His head moved from side to side. His hips began to rise and fall in unison with Xander's efforts.

Xander's hands moved over Sundar's belly, his nipples. He grasped his chin in his hand and his cock pumped out its release, spraying Sundar's belly and chest. Xander threw his head back, his eyes closed tightly as he felt Sundar shoot his come inside of him, providing a soothing calm with a crescendo that was Sundar's deep satisfied groan.

Xander watched him lay back, his head lolling to one side. "You have to get out of here. You're weak."

He didn't say anything else. Xander took the towel he'd brought in and wiped the sweat and come off his body. "Come on," he pulled on him, helping him to stand. He was like a drunk. Xander brought Sundar out of the tent and he seemed to come to life a little. He lowered his head against the bright sunshine.

Sundar reached for the water bottle Xander was holding and drank deeply. He glanced over the landscape and sighed, breathing in the clean fresh air. He wrapped the towel around his waist and glanced at Xander. "What in hell are you doing here?" he demanded.

"Your father sent me."

His eyes widened. "My father?"

"He told me that he had a dream last night. He dreamt that you were here."

"My father had a dream that I was here?"

Xander nodded.

"I find that hard to believe, given that he turned his back on his heritage long ago."

Xander nodded.

"Anyway, you shouldn't have come. Christ. I'm not five years old." He picked up a t-shirt that was laying on a rock.

"Joyce is worried too."

"Joyce?"

"Are you going to marry her after all?"

"Leave me alone with that shit," he muttered, pulling on his t-shirt and searching for his jeans. "Where are my keys?"

"It's just that she was at your mother's and…"

"It's over with Joyce and me. She knows that. She has no business bothering my mother with what happened between us." He began walking in the direction of the house. He had a lot on his mind. He didn't need Xander showing up to complicate things. He froze suddenly, looked around. Xander was right behind him. "Am I nuts, or did we just fuck back there?"

Xander nodded. "You're not nuts."

"You came into a sweat lodge and fucked me? Jesus, Xander."

"Technically, you fucked me, kind of." He looked away.

Sundar kept on walking. "Jesus," he muttered, opening the door to the house. "Running Creek?" he called out as he walked in.

His uncle came out into the kitchen with Sundar's jacket in his hand. "Lose something?"

"Yeah, thanks."

"So?"

"I don't know. Things are rather muddled right now." He took his jacket and searched his pocket for his keys.

"They will be for awhile. It might get clearer soon enough."

"Um, I hope so. Thanks."

"You met your spirit guide."

"The wolf."

"Yep," his uncle nodded. "Say hello to my brother."

Sundar nodded. "Did you know it was him who…"

"Sooner or later, we all go back home," he said abruptly.

Xander was standing by Sophia's car when Sundar came out of the house. Sundar paused, and looked at him. He'd been hoping he'd already left.

"Sundar," Xander said, coming forward and placing a hand on his forearm, "what are you going to do now?"

Sundar met his gaze. "I don't know yet."

"I love you."

"Stop that," he snapped then softened his voice. "I know you do." He took his arm away.

"I don't want to fuck your life up."

"You don't want to give me any space either." He knew he sounded angry again. He got into his car and shut the door.

"Mark told me not to give you space," he glanced at him through the window.

"Fuck Mark," he muttered and put the key in the ignition.

"You did that, remember? That really hurt, Sundar, you fucking Mark."

"I'm sorry." He looked at him. "I'm sorry for a lot of things, Xander. Fucking Mark was just…easier, that's all."

"Because it didn't mean anything."

"Something like that," he muttered. "I got to go."

He drove away without another word, glancing at the rear view once to see that Xander was still standing there, looking miserable. "Damn it," he swore, squealing to a stop. He put the car in reverse and backed up to where Xander was still standing. "Xander?"

Xander bent down and peered in the window. His eyes were shining with unshed tears. "Yeah?"

"Don't take it the wrong way but I really need some time to figure this all out. It doesn't mean I don't...care."

"If I'm not around, you'll marry Joyce, won't you?"

"What are you talking about? I told you we're not getting married. It's over. It was a bad idea. Plus, she deserves better than me."

"You need me around to remind you of what we have, what you need."

"We don't *have* anything."

"That's not true. And you know it. And that's why you fucked Mark. When we're alone, you lose control not only because you want me but because...well you care. And that's all I have to hold onto, although I'm trying so damn hard to let go. I'm not going to let you forget it. I know that I can't let go, even if I slept with my boss."

He swallowed then hit the steering wheel with his fist. "God damn it, Xander. I don't want to hear about Rob."

"You're jealous."

"I am not jealous. Fuck who you want to!"

"That would be you."

"You're impossible," he grumbled and hit the gas again.

Xander watched him go barrelling down the road, dirt flying behind him. Mark had been right. He had to be around to remind Sundar that it was Xander he wanted.

"I'm not giving up on you, baby," he called out, turning to go back to Sophia's car.

The tall man was standing there now, the dog at his side.

Xander was sure he'd heard that. He looked at the ground, embarrassed.

"Sundar needs to find his heart," he said, looking at the trail of dust Sundar had made with the car.

Xander glanced at him. "I think he knows where his heart belongs but he can't accept it."

He said nothing.

"You disapprove?"

"I have no right to judge a man's heart. It's a very private thing. You've already lost yours. Just be careful it doesn't get trampled on."

"You think he'll deny his heart?"

"Depends on if he's got the balls, or not. It's that simple."

"What was the point of that sweat lodge then?"

"It can point the way but you got to have the heart to follow it. Men are particularly good at denying the truth. We've been doing it since time began."

Xander walked to the car and opened the door. "I can make him happy if only he'd let me."

The big man met his gaze. "Then don't let go until you see him reach the edge."

"What does that mean, the edge?"

"He'll need to cling to someone or he'll fall. Anyway, you'll know," he said, slapping the car a few times, "because he's part of you. Have a good trip."

"I want a drink," Sundar told the bartender, "and keep 'em coming." He'd seen his future in that tent. He knew where it lay but the answer didn't give him the peace he sought. He could choose to disregard what he saw, choose another path. "I can make it work," he muttered, swallowing the whisky. "I will make it work." *Make it work with whom? Joyce? Another poor woman you'll use to hide behind? Better to be alone then ruin someone's life.*

"Where is he?" Sophia asked when Xander walked in later that evening.

"Safe. He was with Running Creek."

Sophia glanced at Clint, holding her breath. He said nothing.

"What was he doing there?" Sophia asked.

"He was in the sweat lodge. And I don't think he appreciated being followed. He's a grown man."

"He's still my little boy. And Joyce is worried. I know Joyce will make a wonderful…"

"Sophia," Clint stood up from the table, "for Christ's sake, leave Sundar alone. He is not going to marry that woman."

Her jaw dropped. "Why do you say that? She's a nice girl and…"

Xander was looking at Clint, who came over to stand in front of his wife.

"Any man who goes through that much agony over marriage shouldn't take that walk. I saw Sundar last night in a dream. It was I who sent Xander to find him. My son is lost somehow. He doesn't say much but it's in his eyes."

"You knew about…but Clint…" Sophia protested.

"It's part of who he is. I was wrong to deny him his heritage. I know that now. And Joyce can't save him, Sophia. First, he has to save himself."

Xander pulled out a chair and sat down as Clint left the kitchen and went outside.

"Xander?" Sophia probed. "What was that all about?"

Xander looked up at her. "Don't worry, Sophia. It's complicated, that's all. Sundar will be alright."

Chapter Eight

He wasn't very good at begging. The captain reeled back in his padded leather chair, and didn't say a word as Sundar spoke. "I like my job. I don't want to lose it. I want to come back, concentrate on my job and..."

Roger Colts brought his chair down with a bang. He leant forward and looked him square in the eye. "Joyce put in for a transfer. I okayed it. You broke the no fraternizing rule. It makes everything go to shit. I don't want to lose a damn good detective because of where you put your dick. Do you understand what I'm saying to you, Kingfisher?"

He nodded.

"I don't give a rat's ass where you put your dick, but when you come into this office, you'd better have your dick in your pants and keep it there. Is that clear?"

He nodded. "Yes, sir."

"Now, get out there to your desk and get to work. You're behind on several cases and the other guys have been picking up the slack. Expect a lot of overtime."

Sundar stood.

"And Sundar," he pointed at him, "one more screw up, and you'll be working as a security guard at Crabtree Valley Mall."

That was clear enough. He thanked him and left quietly. He went to his desk and stayed there, ignoring the way others were looking at him. In an office like this, news travelled and gossip was rampant. It would blow over eventually but for now, he'd just keep his mind on his work, and try not to screw up.

He worked nine hours and then stopped by the liquor store, bought some gin, and went home. He drank until he fell asleep in front of the television and went back to the office two hours earlier than usual, determined to show Roger that he'd redeemed himself.

Work would save him.

Joyce hadn't been transferred yet so he was forced to see her. Thankfully, she said hello, and kept going. He could have hugged her for that.

When a body showed up in Lake Johnson, Sundar was elected to head a team to investigate. Although he certainly felt for the guy they'd found in the water — obviously there due to foul play, given the contusions on his body — he was grateful for the distraction. Twelve hours days, without any time off, were good for him. It kept him away from the bottle, but he knew, as they got close to catching the killer, it wouldn't last forever.

Xander was worried that what had happened between him and Rob would affect his progress at the hotel. It was a little awkward especially now they both realised it was over.

He was still working at the desk and Rob was gradually giving him more and more responsibilities. He was relieved when one day as he was getting ready to call it a day; Rob came over and said, "You're doing really well, Xander. You'll make a fine manager one day."

"Thanks," Xander said. "Rob, I'm — "

"Don't," he said. "I can't blame a man for loving another. I just feel badly that here you are, with so much to give, sleeping alone every night. Xander," he said, taking his elbow and leading him around to the small office, "it's been three weeks since you went running after him when he was out there playing Indian or whatever..."

"He wasn't playing Indian," Xander said, irritated. "He is part Native American, and..."

"Okay, sorry, that was insensitive."

Xander was about to add, *and racist*, but he stopped himself.

"I just mean that...he hasn't been around. You haven't seen him, have you?"

Xander shook his head.

"He doesn't feel the same way you do. You need to try and..."

"Get over him?"

Rob nodded.

"Thanks for the advice, Rob. I know you mean well."

"If you ever want to...talk or..."

"Okay." He rubbed his arms for a second then left.

The winter was finally passing them by and spring was in the air. The walk to the house was pleasant this evening and he took his time. He did what he always did when he walked into the yard. He looked for Sundar's car, and like always, there was no sign of it.

Usually Sophia complained when Sundar didn't come around but after Clint had scolded her one night for not treating Sundar like a man, she'd held her tongue.

The three of them ate Sophia's delicious hamburger casserole and they made small talk. It was pleasant enough, but no one mentioned what was really on their mind, which was Sundar.

Xander helped Sophia with the dishes and sat down to watch hockey with Clint for an hour. After that, he headed up to bed as he had to be at the hotel early to supervise breakfast.

He crawled into bed and closed his eyes. Sundar was there with him as he was every night. "Good night, sweetie, I love you," he said out loud before he fell asleep.

* * * *

There was a celebratory mood among the detectives from his squad tonight. They'd caught the killer of the guy they'd found in the lake. The Captain received a personal call from the mayor, congratulating him on his excellent work. The man had been the son of a wealthy family from the next town, and there had been a lot of pressure to resolve the case.

Roger invited the four detectives who'd worked on the case to have a few drinks at the neighbourhood bar they usually frequented.

Everyone was in a good mood, and extremely tired. The three others bragged loudly about how they'd arrived at this and that conclusion while Sundar sat there quietly and sipped his beer.

The captain came and sat beside him. He picked up his own glass and tapped Sundar's with it. "It was you who came up with the final piece of the puzzle that finally solved the case," Roger said in a voice that was drowned out by the others. "Good work, detective."

Sundar smiled faintly. "It was a team effort."

Roger nodded, drank down his beer and got up to leave. "Take two days off, relax a bit."

"I'd prefer not to."

"Is it because Joyce is finally gone? I know there must be some…" he trailed off.

"It's not Joyce. I just need to be working right now."

Roger shrugged. "I get that, but you need a break. Take the two days."

What could he do? "Okay, thanks."

The captain bid his men goodnight, joking about how his wife would have his head if he came home tanked, and left the bar.

A few minutes later, Sundar allowed himself to be drawn into the conversation with the others. They all drank down a few more rounds and their voices grew more boisterous, and they spewed forth a lot of nonsense which Sundar attempted to laugh at.

At one point, bored with the chit chat, Sundar's gaze moved to the bar. He noticed a young man, sitting with his back was to the bar, staring right at him. When he noticed Sundar looking, he raised his glass, and smiled.

Sundar tore his gaze away, and submerged himself back into the conversation, laughing a little too hard at the nonsense that was coming out of the other guys' mouths.

A few minutes later, his gaze moved back to the guy at the bar. He was handsome, boyish looking, fair-haired, with great smile. He looked a little like.…*No. I won't say his name. Forget the guy at the bar, Sundar. Forget him.*

He motioned the bartender for another beer, left the money on the table, and excused himself to go to the bathroom. He didn't look at the guy at the bar as he walked to the can, at least he didn't think he had.

When the door opened as he was washing his hands, he looked up into the mirror to see that guy who'd been sitting at the bar. "Hi," he said, moving over beside him, "I'm Sam."

Xander glanced at him. "Yeah, well I'm drunk, go figure," he laughed, walking over to the hand dryer and pressing it on.

He swallowed as he felt the man step in behind him, close. He could feel his breath on his neck. "I don't know about drunk," he said softly, "but you're one hell of a good looking hunk of man. I could hardly keep my eyes off of you. Want to come home with me? Say yes," he murmured, moving in and taking Sundar's earlobe between his teeth. One hand moved around him and slid up his thigh.

Sundar sucked in some breath and then hastily moved away as the door opened. He breathed a sigh of relief to see that it was some stranger he didn't know, and he took the opportunity to quickly leave the bathroom and go back to his table.

The others were still laughing and talking bullshit and Sundar announced that he was beat and was going to go. He got some flak from the others but he resisted their pleas for him to hang around and headed to the door.

When he got to the parking lot, the first thing he saw was his friend from the bathroom. He was standing next to a vintage Ford from the 60's. "Nice car," he said. How could he not comment on a beauty like that?

"Nice Camaro," the guy tossed his head towards Sundar's vehicle. "69?"

He nodded, putting the key in the door. He glanced at him over the top. "Very good."

"I am," he drawled, "very good."

Sundar felt his cock stiffen. He licked his lips. "Really?"

"Yeah," he walked over to the passenger side of the Camaro. "Want to give me a ride?"

Yeah, I want to give you a ride. "Ah, you have a car," he laughed a little.

"69, did you consciously pick that year?"

"Are you trying to make some sexual innuendo about my car?" His gaze was now meeting his.

"No. Just a question."

"I liked the car, wasn't that concerned about the year."

"Oh. So, where are we going? My place or yours?"

Sundar sucked in some breath and turned the key in the lock. He opened the door and slid in. The guy was still standing on the other side, waiting. Sundar pressed the button and the door unlocked then opened. The guy slipped into the seat beside him. He looked at him, smiled. "Hi."

Sundar smiled back. "Hi."

"I'm only in town for the night. I have a room two blocks from here at the Carolina Cove."

Life was just filled with irony. "Nice place."

"It has a bed." His hand reached over to rest on Sundar's thigh.

Sundar started the engine.

* * * *

194

As far as Xander was concerned, only birds should be awake at four o'clock in the morning, but that's the time he had to be up if he was going to be at the hotel by five. As it was, he was a few minutes late, but Rob wasn't there, and he knew no one would squeal on him.

Anyway, the staff was doing fine without him. Rob had a knack of hiring good people, and they were hard working for the most part and reliable. "Did you eat yet?" Anita asked him, starting the coffee.

"I had a banana."

She laughed. "Try the chef's waffles. They're fabulous," she said.

The chef eyed him now, a plump very temperamental fellow who didn't like to be watched. "I'm going to check on something. I'll be back. Hank is giving me the evil eye."

Anita laughed. "He's harmless."

"Great chefs are always volatile," Seth said, the guy who got all the crappy kitchen work. He was peeling potatoes and throwing them into a big pot of water. "It's passion!"

Xander laughed and left the kitchen. Hank had enough passion for all of them. He checked his watch. It was time for Sandra to go home. She had been at the desk all night. When he got to the lobby, she was checking out a couple, and the bellhop, a guy called Peter, was wheeling their bags outside to wait for the shuttle to the airport.

"They left early," Xander said, smiling at Sandra.

"Early flight, going to Paris," she sighed. "Lucky."

He smiled at her. "You should go home. I'll stay here until Tamara comes on at seven."

"Okay," she said, getting her things together. "See you tonight."

"Bye, Tammy," he said as he moved in behind the desk.

It was quiet at this time of morning. Check out didn't usually get busy until about eight. He turned on the computer and checked the headlines on the home page for a few minutes, looking up when he heard the elevator open at the lobby. His eyes widened when he saw Sundar coming out of the elevator. *Was in the hell is he doing here?*

Sundar looked just as stunned to see him. "Hello, Xander," he said, slowing down as he approached the desk. "I didn't realise you worked so early in the morning."

"I...I'm supervising the...what are you doing here?"

He looked scrumptious, if not a little rumpled. He was wearing a suit, collar open, tie peaking out of his suit jacket. His dark hair was still damp. Obviously he'd just gotten out of the shower a little while ago. "I, ah...was visiting."

"Visiting?"

"Xander, don't complicate this."

"Complicate?" He shook his head. "You brought a man here to this hotel, where I work?"

"You see—you're taking it as a personal insult. I didn't bring him here. He...brought me here." He shoved his hands in his pocket.

Xander was shaking. "Why?"

"It just happened, and I don't owe you a fucking explanation."

Xander watched as Sundar stalked across the floor, slammed his hand on the glass door and left the hotel.

"Wow." The bellhop came back inside after smoking a cigarette outside. "Who's the hostile guest?"

Xander sighed. "Doesn't matter. He won't be coming back here. Do you know what room that guy was in?"

"Nope, didn't see him at all. Was he registered?"

Xander shook his head. "He was a guest of someone."

"Aren't they supposed to pay extra?"

"Yeah, but it's too late now."

"Oh, I get it," Peter said, laughing. "That guy was a gigolo, and he spent the night with some older woman up in a suite. Maybe she didn't pay him."

Xander nodded sickly and turned away. A range of emotions flooded over him—anger, jealousy, sadness and frustration—frustration that Sundar would spend the night with another man, rather than come to him.

Sundar finally came to a stop five blocks away from the hotel. He didn't realise that he'd been practically running. He was totally out of breath. His car was still parked in the parking lot under the hotel. He rested his hand on the telephone post for a moment then headed back to the hotel, this time walking at a leisurely pace.

He'd spent last night in bed with a stranger, a stranger whose name he still didn't know. He'd spent the night fucking one man and dreaming about another. Is this what his life had come to?

There had been such pain on Xander's face when he'd seen him come off that elevator. That's what he couldn't take, what propelled him to practically run away from him, leaving his car behind.

He paused in front of the underground parking lot, intending to go to get his car but instead, he walked back into the lobby.

Xander was there, still at the front desk. He looked at him strangely, probably wondering what in fuck he was doing back here.

Sundar walked up to the desk. He swallowed. He felt hot and feverish. He was perspiring from the run he'd just taken. "Xander," he said. "I don't want to be the one…" he stopped, finding it hard to speak. He looked around to see if anyone was looking at him. "I don't want..."

"I know," Xander said bitterly. "You don't want me. You've made that more than clear when..."

"No," he shook his head, "it's not what I want to say. Give me a chance."

Xander nodded. "Go on."

"I don't want to be the one to put that look on your face, to give you pain. I can't..." he lowered his head, "I can't..." he shook his head, turned and walked blindly to the door.

"Sundar!" Xander called out, coming out from behind the desk, but just as he was about to go after him, Rob came through the door.

Sundar bumped right into him. He raised his head, looked at him a second then continued on out the door.

Xander stood helplessly in the middle of the lobby while Rob stood staring at him.

"Was that...? What was he doing here?"

Xander shook his head. "It was a mistake," he said. "He came to tell me something about his mother and..." He felt a tear run down his cheek.

Rob took him by the arm and steered him towards the office. "Are you alright? Did that bastard hurt you?"

"Not in the way you think."

"Tell me," Rob urged.

"He spent the night here with another man," he lowered his head, blinking to squeeze off some of the water in his eyes then wiped it away. "I'm sorry."

"Xander, you've got to forget him. He's no good for you."

Xander nodded. "I know."

"Look, go home. Take the rest of the day off. We'll be okay without you today."

"No, I can't let you…"

"Xander, go on," Rob insisted. "It will be okay."

"Why in hell can't I be in love with you?" Xander asked and hugged him briefly.

Rob gave him a sad look. "Maybe in time?"

Xander smiled faintly. "You never know."

* * * *

A few minutes later, Xander was walking back to the house. If only Rob hadn't come into the hotel when he did, maybe Sundar would have opened up to him a little more. He'd seemed so upset, and Xander wasn't sure what in hell was going on inside of him. Sundar had looked as if he wanted to talk, really talk.

Xander paused a few blocks from the house. He pulled out his cell phone and called for a cab. When the cab pulled up at the corner, Xander gave him Sundar's home address. He had to see him. They had to talk.

When his doorbell rang, Sundar raised his face from his hands and got to his feet. He narrowed his eyes as he approached the door. He sure as hell wasn't in the mood for company. He hoped he hadn't told that guy last night where he lived.

When he pulled open the door and saw Xander standing there, he didn't know what to feel. Part of him was so happy to see him that he almost threw his arms around him, the other part of him was in avoidance mode. "I'm in no mood for a fight," he said, leaving the door open.

Xander came in and closed it. "I didn't come to fight."

"What did you come for then?"

There was silence.

"Well?" Sundar persisted.

"I could say I came to fuck," Xander said, meeting his gaze.

Sundar swallowed.

"Or, I could say that I came to talk, which was my original intention but Jesus Christ, Sundar...." He started towards him.

Sundar met him half way.

Xander took his face in between both hands and kissed him hotly while Sundar dragged him closer to his body. "Sundar, oh Sundar," Xander moaned against him as Sundar scrambled to take off Xander's clothes and his own at the same time.

Xander mustered the courage to pull away from Sundar for a few minutes to take off his shirt and get his pants off. He kicked off his shoes then stumbled over his pants and underwear while he pushed Sundar backwards to the bedroom and fumbled with the zipper on his blue pants.

By the time they both slammed against the bedroom door, knocking something off Sundar's bureau that was of no immediate importance, they were both naked except for their socks.

Xander kissed Sundar's neck as he held his erection in his palm and caressed it with the fingers of his other hand.

They fell together on the bed, Xander on top, his mouth immediately zeroing in on Sundar's chest. He licked a trail down his stomach and then enthusiastically took his cock into his mouth as he knelt between Sundar's open thighs.

"Yes, yes," Sundar urged, his hands in Xander's fair hair. He pulled slightly as Xander moved his lips up and down Sundar's shaft, one hand cupping his balls at the same time.

Sundar reached down for Xander's other hand and he entwined their fingers.

Xander smiled inside as he continued to work on Sundar's cock. *I love you so much. God damn it, Sundar, I love you.*

Sundar was coming, his hips lifting off the mattress. He whimpered then gasped, and grunted a few times.

Xander slid his body up on top of his, taking his mouth, French kissing him hotly. "God, I want you to fuck me," he urged, taking Sundar's hand and placing it on his cock. "I'm so hard."

Sundar stroked his hair and gently rolled Xander off of him. He looked down into his eyes, his fingers caressing Xander's shaft. *Love.* He saw love in those eyes and Sundar felt his cock stiffen again. Was there any greater turn on than this?

He pulled Xander up into his arms and kissed his mouth, his neck. He didn't move for a minute, experiencing the feeling of holding him.

"Sundar?" Xander's voice was curious. "Are you all right?"

"I am now," he whispered. His lips moved now across Xander's chest. He swiped his tongue around the head of Xander's cock and was rewarded with a loud groan. He smiled and lifted Xander's legs, his fingers finding their way to his anus.

"You plan on torturing me first?" Xander grunted.

"You bet," he smiled, abruptly flipping his legs up on to his shoulders so that he could tease his entrance with his tongue.

Xander was reacting exactly the way Sundar intended him to, squirming and gasping. "Um…Sundar, God, stop…stop…I can't…fuck me…please."

Sundar leant over and took some lube out of the night stand. He hastily squirted some on his fingers then pushed two fingers up inside of him.

"Oh my…ahhh….baby…go…go…"

Sundar fucked him a little with his fingers, his tongue wetting his lips as he thought about how good it was going to be, to be inside his ass. Xander's head was back, eyes closed and his cock was already dripping with cum. "Fuck me," he gasped, pushing Sundar back and turning onto his stomach.

Sundar didn't hesitate. He grabbed his hips and knocked everything off his side table, including the drawer of his night stand, trying to put his hands on a condom. His hands shaking, he ripped off the top and rolled the rubber onto his erection.

Xander cried out something when Sundar drilled his cock into him. It sounded like he said…*it's okay now*, but he couldn't be sure. Sundar lowered his lips to Xander's neck and kissed him as he pulled him upwards and pounded him with his cock. It felt as if he hadn't fucked in years, when actually he'd fucked last night with that stranger.

He stopped thinking suddenly. He was coming and he reached around and pulled on Xander's cock, which felt as if it was already half way there, and his entire body gave way to orgasm. "Ah, ah…ahhhhhhh…." He wasn't sure if that was him or Xander, or maybe both of them together. He held on tight, his body relaxing, drained, his sweaty head pressing against Xander's. "I love you."

He was lying on his back now staring at the ceiling, every muscle in his body relaxed. It was raining outside. He could hear the raindrops beating on the window. It made the room darker without the sun.

A hand slipped into his. He took it without comment and closed his eyes.

Xander reared up now on his elbow.

Sundar opened his eyes and Xander was looking down into his eyes.

"You said that you loved me. You can't take it back now." His voice was low, even.

"Was that me?" It was an honest question.

Xander nodded.

He cleared his throat.

Xander gently wiped at his cheek with his fingers. "You're crying."

"Am I?"

"Are you going to answer every question with a question?" He obviously tried to make light of it, but it didn't come off that way. There was too much emotion in Xander's voice.

"What should I do now, go home and pretend again that this never happened, that you never said that? And don't say, 'should you?'."

"No." He tightened his grip on his hand. "No more pretending."

Xander stroked his hair. "I love you too."

He nodded. "I know." He smiled and lifted his head for a kiss.

Xander kissed him then stayed there, hovering above him.

"In that sweat lodge, I saw your face. I was trying to make my way over this rough terrain. It was hard, very treacherous, and I knew that at the end, someone waited for me. It was your face I saw and then, there you were, with me in the tent." He sighed, opened his arms and dragged Xander down into them. "I have to be who I am. I know that but it's so damn hard. All my life, I've lived like a straight white man, when the truth is; I'm neither straight, nor white. And you know what?" He turned his face to Xander's and smiled, "I'm glad."

Xander kissed him and said, "You don't have to tell everyone you're gay if..."

"Look, I've decided not to hide it anymore. It's going to tough and I'm not saying I'm going to go around shouting it from the rooftops, but if someone asks, I won't deny it. And I won't deny you. Stay with me, Xander. Come and live with me here."

Xander smiled and nodded. He hugged him close. "Oh Sundar, you've made me the happiest guy on earth."

Sundar kissed the top of his head. "Feeling is mutual, sweetheart, feeling is mutual."

* * * *

That night before Sundar went to work, he drove Xander by his parent's house.

Xander was surprised when he got out of the car with him. "I thought you were going to work?"

"I have something I have to do first," he said, placing an arm around Xander's shoulders. "Come on."

It was Xander who was nervous. Sundar seemed to be very calm and peaceful. Xander wondered if he wasn't responsible for pushing him a little too fast. "You don't need to tell your folks just yet," Xander said.

"Yes, I do," he said. "It's time. Just let me do this," he took a breath.

Xander nodded and walked into the house.

"Mom," Sundar called out walking down the hallway with Xander. He reached for his hand as he got to the kitchen.

Both his parents were sitting at the table, mugs of tea in front of them. They'd been playing cards. They looked up as they came in.

Sundar clutched Xander's hand tighter.

"Sundar," Sophia said, a smile on her face, "I'm happy to see you. Are you on your way to work?" Her eyes went to Sundar's hand which was tightly bound to Xander's.

"Yeah," he said. "Hello, Dad."

Clint got up from the table and left the room.

Xander's heart fell. This wasn't going to be easy.

Sophia looked confused then noticed that Sundar was holding Xander's hand. Before she could say anything, Sundar said, "Mom, I've been trying to pretend that I was straight for many years, but I guess I knew in high school that I was gay. Xander is my lover. We met before he came here, and I was foolish enough to turn him away because I didn't..." His voice broke. "I was a coward. Now, I'm telling you who I am. I'm the same man I always was, except Xander and I are now together. Either you accept me or don't, but..."

Sophia crossed the kitchen and threw her arms around Sundar.

Xander let go of his hand to give them some space.

"My baby," she cried. "I'll always love you no matter what and..."

"Sundar," a voice said suddenly.

They looked to see Clint standing there. He was holding an elaborate Native headdress in his hand.

Sophia placed a hand on her heart, and Sundar took a step towards his father. "What is it?" he asked.

"It belonged to your great grandfather who was the chief of his tribe. This was his. My father gave it to me as the eldest son, and now it is yours. You are finally ready to accept it."

Sundar took it in his hands and studied it carefully. "It's beautiful." He looked at his father. "Thank you."

Clint nodded. "Now, if you don't mind," he grumbled, "I was in the process of beating your mother quite nicely at a hand of gin rummy." He sat back down. "Come on, woman; get back to your cards."

Sundar's eyes were bright with tears but he didn't say anything. He turned and smiled at Xander. "I got to go to work. Can you take care of this for me?"

Xander nodded. "Sure."

"I suppose," Sophia said, studying her cards, "you'll be taking Xander away now?"

Sundar smiled at Xander. "Yeah."

"You're finding us a new roommate," she grumbled, throwing down a card which Clint beat. "Damn it."

"I'll put out the word."

"Your mother has got all kinds of junk in the basement she doesn't need," Clint said, taking possession of two more cards and banging his fist on the table with joy.

"Clint," Sophia was saying as Xander walked Sundar down the hallway to the front door, "you're always looking for a way for me to give away all my…"

They were outside now, Xander holding the headdress and Sundar glancing up at the stars. "That wasn't so bad," Xander said, kissing his cheek.

"Maybe I was the last one to know."

Xander smiled and hugged him.

"That was the easy part. I got the people at work yet. Not sure how they're going to take to a gay cop."

"You'll still be able to kick ass," Xander joked.

"That I will, babe," Sundar chuckled, giving him a quick kiss and walking to his car.

Xander watched him drive away, and for the first time, he didn't have that feeling of dread. They'd see each other soon, and no matter what they had to face in the future, whatever ignorance and prejudice was out there, they'd face it together.

Sundar drove towards the police station with a smile on his face. Everything looked new to him, fresh, and that heavy cloud which hung over him finally was gone. He promised himself he'd visit his uncle more often, and maybe he could even get his father to go with him. He wanted to know the stories of his ancestors. They were a part of him, a part that was waiting to be discovered. Xander would take care of the rest. From now on, he'd be there when he opened his eyes and again when he closed them. Love would surround him, and finally make him whole.

About the Author

I write not only for my own pleasure, but for the pleasure of my readers. I can't remember a time in my life when I haven't written and told stories. When I'm not writing, I'm dreaming about writing. Eroticism between consenting adults, in all its many forms is the icing on the cake of life but one does not live by sex alone. The story of how two people find love in spite of the odds is what really turns me on.

D.J. Manly loves to hear from readers. You can find her contact information, website details and author profile page at http://www.total-e-bound.com.

Total-E-Bound Publishing

www.total-e-bound.com

Take a look at our exciting range of literagasmic™
erotic romance titles and discover pure quality
at Total-E-Bound.